My Virtual Life

By

Sharon Dempsey

GW00360857

Also by Sharon Dempsey:

Little Bird
A Posy of Promises

For Kate, Owen and Sarah

Chapter 1
Shoeless and rat-faced

Stella

I'm throwing my hands in the air in that raver way. Trying to look cool when really I'd love to be dancing to a bit of Bon Jovi or ABBA. Maybe they'll do a remix of 'Mamma Mia' and they'll all be so out of their heads that they'll think it's hilarious. I need a fag break so bad, but at least all this jumping around like a loon is burning calories.

I make the universal fag-break sign to Elaine and make my way out to the decking. The garden is strung up with threads of fairy lights all twinkling and looking like something straight out of *Homes and Gardens* magazine. Huge planters stand on either side of the decking and pretty white flowers cascade downwards giving off a delicate scent. There is a configuration of rattan sofas and oversized bean bags where the most beautiful people have arranged themselves, as if in anticipation of the perfect photo. Instagram ready.

Everybody knows all the best craic goes on in the smoking garden. Right Stella, look cool, nonchalant is the word. Smokers' huddles are always so exclusive.

I'll just light up and lean back against this wall and contemplate life and stuff.

The sky is studded with diamonds. It's so pretty I could cry. It makes me feel insignificant, you know? Like that I'm just a speck of nothingness. The thought of the vastness of it all terrifies me. I look across the garden and see little clusters of people. I'm smiling to make sure I have a faraway look, as if I'm remembering a cute joke someone has just told me. I don't want to look like I'm bored when really I'd love to be home watching *Love Island*, but I can't give in to that stay-at-home mentality. I'll never meet anyone that way; besides, I can't exactly take a selfie of myself slobbing out on the sofa with the remote control in my hand. It would be different if I could persuade Tara to watch *Love Island* with me. Then we could orchestrate a little photo opportunity, lean in for one and pretend we are having mother and daughter time, but fat chance of her agreeing to that. I don't understand her reluctance to embrace social media. It's as if she has been sent forth from the Victorian age in a time machine. God, I'm really pissed. Focus Stella! Don't let yourself become overwhelmed. Moderation is the name of the game.

The problem is I have to be seen to be out and about enjoying myself and keeping up with the young ones. It's so hard, you know? The struggle is real.

One more drink for the road won't hurt. It's Sunday tomorrow. A day of rest. Maybe Tara and I can do a lazy brunch day. Yes, that would be lovely. We could go somewhere cute like Miel et Moi and take pics of our French toast, drizzled with maple syrup beside our flat whites.

***

There's a pneumatic drill hammering somewhere close by and I can hear a fire alarm too. I try to open my eyes but the eyelash glue seems to have jammed them together. I'm going to have bald eyelids again. Great.

I need my phone to check the time. Christ! It's almost dawn. How da feck did that happen? Must have fallen asleep and missed the party. Oh, wait, I'm still at the party. That noise – sweet Jesus, it would wreck your head altogether. Oh dear God – it is *music*. Some club sound that only works if you take the magic beans and I can't touch them. Not after the last time. Tara would kill me.

Tara. Christ the night! My blasphemy is getting worse. How do I sneak home at this hour? She's bound to hear me. I don't think I could bear one of her glares over the breakfast table. There's a particular look she gives that makes me feel like the worst mother ever when really, I'm quite good. I'd never leave her home alone. That's what Kveta is for. I pay her salary, don't I? At least I do when I remember.

I'm a little bit sober now. Sober enough to function in that small window of opportunity before the hangover kicks in. I need to move but my legs don't seem to be cooperating. It's as if they're still asleep. Shoes, I need shoes. Where did I leave them? Oh, there's one in my handbag, that's good. Forward thinking on my part, excellent. Now the other one. Where could it be? Think, Stella, think! Where was the after party? Sammy, the producer's house. Good, so I'm in Belfast. That's something. Not too far to make it home, though I'd rather be doing it with two shoes instead of one. If only my eyes would unglue it would be of help. I'm going to have to pick the glue off bit by bit. Ouch. It hurts. One eye will do. Marvellous, I see a shoe. It may not be mine, but it'll have to do.

**

It's a little while later when I hear, 'Mum, you said we could do something today. It's gone ten and you're still in bed.'

'Tara, please, I just need another few minutes. I'm not feeling so good. Period pains, you know?'

She makes that face, the one she saves for any time I mention sexual organs, menstruation, menopause or pregnancy. I think she's an android, devoid of bodily functions. The door closes with a sharp click. I might have bought myself another half hour.

I'm desperate to stay in bed, so next time she comes in I'll suggest a *Gilmore Girls* marathon TV session. That way I can stay cosied up and hopefully Tara won't mind too much if I drift off to sleep.

Tara

It's Sunday afternoon. Stella has declared a duvet day – code for hung-over – so we are snuggled up in bed watching *Gilmore Girls* for the hundredth time. The scarlet red, zany patterned Pip Studio duvet cover is scattered with Pringle crumbs and a couple of Nutella stains. There is a packet of Nurofen on the bedside cabinet, a half-drunk glass of Berocca and a pair of sunglasses. A wire mannequin stands guard in the corner of the room wearing fluffy angel wings and a marabou snood. Clothes are scattered across the floor where Stella has tried them on and discarded them the night before, dropping them as she goes. The dressing table looks like it has been used by a theatre production company: make-up, lotions, glittery eyeshadows and nail polishes in every shade of red imaginable, fight for space amongst silver chains, crystal belts and feathery earrings.

We've reached the part were Lorelai is retelling Rory the story of her birth and for some reason it's making me emotional. I glance up at Stella to see if she is feeling the moment too, but she is sound asleep with her mouth open and a snail trail of saliva creeping down her chin. Not for the first time, I wish Lorelai was my real mum. She may be kooky, she may believe that 'five a day' refers to the number of coffees you should drink at Luke's diner before lunch, and she may not be the most sensible of mums, but compared to mine, she is picture-book perfect. Mother envy is a thing.

Stella emits a soft snozzily snore, while on screen Lorelai tells Rory she's a great kid and the best friend a girl could ever have. I sigh.

But Stella is home. We have breakfasted on Nutella and toasted bagels, lunched on cheese and chive Pringle sandwiches, and snacked on honey-roasted peanuts.

From the depths of the duvet I hear, 'Wha' time's it?'

The creature lives.

'Quarter past four.'

Stella

The next time I wake, it's dark. Proper dark. Middle of the night dark. I listen but all is quiet and still. My phone lights up and tells me it's 1.37am. Shit! I slept all day. God, why am I such a bad mother? The cold sweat of self-loathing is upon me. Maybe it's early menopause? I hate myself. I really do!

My mouth feels like the inside of my old Louis Vuitton handbag. I need water and sustenance. Where's Tara when I need her? A good daughter would have had the forethought to have left some Nurofen, a bottle of icy water and some crisps on my bedside table. It looks like she's cleared up. There's nothing else for it. I'll have to go and administer to my own hangover.

On my way downstairs, I open her bedroom door slightly. There she is, sound asleep. Her mouth is open in a beautiful little 'o', looking just the way she used to when she was a baby. She breathes slowly and deeply and looks so peaceful. God,

I love that girl so much my heart wells up with the emotion of it. I can never do enough or be good enough for her, no matter how hard I try. It only seems like a few years ago I was pacing the floors, with her squawking her head off, her little mouth an angry grimace. Even then she looked at me as if telling me I wasn't worthy of her. She came out whip smart and could see straight through to my sorry soul.

Baby girl, I'd do anything for you, I wish you knew that.

I close the door and go in search of salty carbs and a bottle of cold water.

Chapter 2

Lonely Girl Blog

Tara
Age: 14

Occupation: Student of life
Interests: Watching vlogs, reading, taking pics and drawing

Listening to: Two Door Cinema Club, Twenty-One Pilots, Imagine Dragons, Panic at the Disco, Ed Sheeran (but don't tell Stella).

Reads: The Hunger Games (team Peeta), Patrick Ness, most Neil Gaiman, and Gerard Durrell's My Family and Other Animals, sometimes re-reading Enid Blyton books but ironically. All John Greene, I Capture the Castle by Dodie Smith.

Collecting: Gel pens and nice notebooks from Paperchase.

Watching: Reruns of Gilmore Girls. Love, love, love Gilmore Girls, but I hate Luke's annoying sister. And why did poor Lane have to get pregnant? Also selected Ted Talks. The Handmaid's Tale in an effort to educate Stella on gender politics, Riverdale, The Good Life, Alex Strangelove.

Hobbies: Drawing and scribbling stories, collecting gel pens and nice notebooks from Paperchase. There is something magical about shopping for stationery. All those rows of pretty pens and swanky notebooks with fresh creamy pages to be scrawled on is bliss to me.

Fav films: Classics like ET, Lost Boys and Boy in the Striped Pyjamas, Coraline.

Relationship status: Negotiable if You Tuber Daniel Howell is interested, also sort of like Brooklyn Beckham when he has his Nikon round his neck.

Pet hates: Usually my mother, girls who use straighteners to straighten their already straight hair and egg sandwiches with watercress.

Like to eat: Chocolate cake, carrot cake, muffins, Subway meatball sandwiches and lasagne, Maltesers dipped in herbal tea.

Ambition: To pen graphic novels.

Kind of have a girl crush on: Tavi and Caitlin Moran, Scarlett Curtis, Malala, Cara Delevingne and Taylor Swift, though my relationship with Swifty is complicated.

Little-known fact: Father not mentioned, ever.

This blog is for the purpose of venting my thoughts, which whirl round and round in my head until I think I'll explode and splatter my bedroom with bits of brain and blood. If I were to see a psychiatrist they would most definitely tell me to keep a journal; to write about my experiences in the hope of finding cathartic release. Failing that, this will be evidence of the life I endured should I decide I must vacate the premises. I wouldn't really, just saying. If I were beautiful, or pretty, or at least not self-conscious and introverted, this would be a vlog instead of a blog. It is what it is. Read, or don't read. Comment, or don't comment. I am doing it for the pleasure of documenting my thoughts, not for validation.

Perverts - do not leave comments or pretend to be fourteen-year-old girls trying to befriend me – I know your game and I will report you to Interpol.

Tara
Ruination, humiliation and raspberry red embarrassment
Wednesday 5.56pm

Food consumed since dinner: cherry cheesecake, one slice; oatmeal cookie x 3; one glass of banana and mango smoothie and half an apple.

My mother has damaged me yet again. Over a feast of a breakfast in Molly Malone's (scrambled eggs, hash browns, pancakes and Belfast brewed tea) she suggests, all innocent like, that maybe it's time I had my first wax. I still have a piece of scrambled egg lodged in my windpipe as a result of the choking incident that ensued.

Now I'm sitting in the bathroom examining my hairy bits. It's not pretty, but the feminist in me wants to accept and love my body for what it is, while the susceptible woman that I am looks in the mirror and sees someone resembling an ewok. An hour ago I would have stroked the faint downy hairs on my legs without judgement but now, thanks to my mother, I see coarse badger hair that needs to be eradicated at all cost.

There is nothing else for it but to refer to the bible of all that is holy in modern day feminism and see what Caitlin Moran's *How to Be a Woman* says on the subject. I'll do my research and then make an informed choice.

My mother is home from work. That doesn't mean much in the average person's world, but since my mother's office is in Dublin, her presence at home is worth noting. For most of the week her presence in my life is virtual, i.e. she texts, she phones, she emails me and on one occasion she face timed me to help me with homework.

She has arrived home with this mad glint in her eye that tells me she expects me to run to her, tell her how much I missed her and then spend the next three hours listening to her talk about herself.

I have tried. I promise you I have really tried to read my mother's stupid, brain-dead magazine with an objective eye. But the neon bright colours and the manic italicised print are practically screaming at me and it is doing my head in. I would be at risk of developing a migraine if I were that type of person.

The sentences are short and pithy, like little mantras for the masses, to be repeated until they are lodged in their feeble little brains for future reference.

For those of you lucky enough to not know what I am talking about, I shall give you a breakdown of *Heart* magazine:

- There is the obligatory celebrity news. The WAG section. (*Are they implying that the footballers' wives are dog-like appendages?*)
- Updates on the A-list movie stars with their babies clinging on to them like little monkeys in impossibly spotless clothes looking sweet and well behaved. Who's heading for 'splitsville', who is trying to adopt yet another photogenic orphan, who is hooking up with whom. Do celebrities never date civilians?
- The pop stars with their latest boyfriends or girlfriends, tour updates and forthcoming CD releases and the soap actors holding on to whichever TV award they had just won. So far, so boring.

Then there is the *how to* section: how to snog with braces; how to ditch an uncool mate; how to tell a bezzie mate that they have bad breath.

How nice.

God, who reads this rubbish?

I flick on. 'Go Green, Not Mean' sings the next headline. The feature is trying to sell eco-friendly living as a way of showing off green savvy while not being a 'recycle skinflint' as they put it.

Oh no, I have just turned to the double-page spread and there it is: 'Stella's Star Guide to Fashion'. A photo of my *mum* looking ridiculously young staring out at me. I know enough about magazine publishing to realise that she has been airbrushed to within a millimetre of reality to remove any trace of the fact that she is a real live woman. Horror upon horrors that she should actually look like a *mother*!

Give me a sec—

Right, I'm back. On close examination of the offending picture I have found:

1. The fine lines which crinkled up when she laughs have been magically erased.
2. The frown line between her overly arched eyebrows which, according to the depth of its crease, indicates whether she is cross or puzzled has been banished.
3. The little dark mole which normally sits under her right eye has been conveniently obliterated.
4. Even her nose seems to have been lengthened and smoothed out so that it resembles a manipulated piece of Play-Doh.
5. I think they may have trimmed a little of her jaw line.

But worse, much worse than her appearance, is the outfit. If Stella 'Fashion editor for hot teens everywhere' wasn't my mother it would be funny, but instead it is pathetic and sad.

Surely social services should be alerted. I shouldn't have to face this ritual humiliation without counselling of some description.

In the double-page spread my mother is wearing a tiny baby pink tank vest emblazoned with a shower of diamanté studs. Stella stands posed in the full-length photograph with her hand placed on her hip which is jutting out at an unnatural angle, her long legs clad in skin-tight dark jeans, and balancing on ridiculously high platform wedges. Oversized sunglasses (or sunnies as she calls them) sit high on her head and her honey blonde hair is tousled and tweaked to look like she has just effortlessly blown in from the street.

Not for the first time, I can feel the flush of red-hot shame when contemplating my mother's attire.

Why can't she be like Matt's mum, Rae, who wears comfy jeans teamed with cardigans out of Hobbs or Phase Eight and jaunty, spotty scarves from Accessorize? Rae wouldn't be seen dead in any of Stella's clothes. Her freckly snub nose would wrinkle up in distaste but she would never say anything critical. But then again, she wouldn't have to. Any full-grown woman with a smidgen of self-respect and maturity would not want to dress like a spivvy teenager.

I better read it in the hope that it won't somehow identify Stella as my mother. I would happily deny all knowledge of ever having met the new fashion writer of the hottest teen magazine around. Except mummy dearest has blabbed to anyone who would listen, including sending an email from my computer to everyone on my contacts list, announcing her appointment and promising to secure ten per cent off subscriptions for any of my friends. The joke is on her since, beyond Matt, I don't really have any friends and I can't see Matt taking out a subscription any time soon.

My contacts list happened to include Jessica Bailey and Freya Layton who, having once befriended me when I arrived fresh faced from London, have long since moved on up the ranks of grammar school popularity; leaving me firmly behind in the cold shadow of the outcast tree.

Within a week they had discovered that, despite having lived in London, the only thing of interest about me was my accent and that I was neither hip nor happening. I was promptly dropped from the ever-so-temporary echelons of popularity and resigned myself to the familiar and comfortable position of being a school nobody. It is a position I wear with quiet pride and had grown used to in London (not that I had a choice).

Why change the habit of a lifetime?

The outcast tree is a huge sycamore which, for reasons unknown, has become the gathering ground for those not cool enough to hang around the back of the school canteen where sneaky ciggies and clandestine encounters are rumoured to occur. I think it is mainly Year 11s who do all the ciggie sneaking and flirting, though I have it on good authority from Matt that some Year 10s and even odd uber-cool Year 9 have been sighted. Perhaps when I have reached the grand old age of being a Year 11 I will find out what goes on behind the canteen. Until then I shall just have to use my imagination, or more likely Matt's.

Hang on a minute, I just want to read it properly.

'Try adding a flash of florals to your wardrobe this summer.'

'Wear your denim with an edge – go tight, tight, tight!!!'

'Lime green is so hot, team it with lemons and sorbet pinks.'

Please, I ask you, how can someone believe that this stuff is *important*?

At least I can't be actually identified beyond sharing a surname with my mother. But this town is small and Stella's network is overactive in sharing its gossip. Besides, she is so into herself for landing this job that she is telling anyone and everyone about it. Last week she stopped some random girl in the middle of Great Victoria Street and told her that her wide brown belt was 'to die for'. Of course, she just had to go on to explain her 'professional interest' as if the girl would be at all impressed. Unfortunately, the randomer was the type of air-brain twit to think writing for a fashion magazine was cool and asked Stella for her autograph. How ridiculous! Stella then gushed about the incident all day. She thinks she is famous now.

10.13pm

Perhaps it is some sort of elaborate April Fool's prank. But if it is, knowing my mum, she would have a TV company lined up to record my horrified reaction. Then everyone at school and beyond would be able to view me again and again as my face explodes into a crushed raspberry red mess of embarrassment.

Maybe I could go to every newsagent between here and school and buy every copy of *Heart* before anyone else gets their hands on it. But that would mean spending every penny I have saved for the last three months and I would look like a spacer buying hundreds of copies of that stupid magazine.

Sorry to go on about this but I am traumatised. How am I supposed to go to school knowing certain people will have bought the offending publication and identified Stella Hunter, 'Fashion editor for hot teens everywhere', as my mother. Is there no justice in the world? Have I not endured enough shamefaced scorn as the result of the huge evolutionary biological joke of being my mother's daughter?

There is nothing for it but to accept that my life is over.

I can't hope to make any sort of come back from this humiliation. My mother, 'Fashion editor for hot teens everywhere', has ruined my life, yet again.

How my mother has ruined my life – part one
Thursday 6.56pm

Food consumed since came home from school: one Petits Filous (i.e. one six pack), one flapjack peanut butter sandwich (trust me, it is worth the mess), one glass of pineapple juice. Dinner was Quorn sausages (don't know why as no one in this house is a veggie) with frozen mash (obviously it wasn't frozen when I ate it).

Lonely Girl Blog

Please note that I am not a saddo no-mates person. I have BFFs, or at least I have Matt who I have known since forever – well, nearly two years. He is funny, clever and annol ying, usually all at once. My problem is that, as he is male and I am female, there are certain issues that we cannot converse on. My mother is one of them.

1. She got pregnant without being married at the age of eighteen and then refused to stay with my father.
2. She decided to go travelling throughout Central America when I was less than a year old, taking me with her and putting me at risk of malaria, typhoid and severe sunburn. All of which probably caused my phobia of needles since I had to have several vaccinations against said tropical diseases.

3. She dressed me in unimaginably cringeworthy clothes throughout my childhood – try wearing a pink tutu with a skull and crossbones motif, striped pirate top, teamed with miniature Doc Marten boots when you are six. She thought I looked cute; I looked demented. The other kids at reception class were frightened of me.
4. She thinks it's okay to wander around the house in her underwear and doesn't understand that when the bathroom door is closed it is because I want privacy.
5. She likes to eat her favourite Ben and Jerry's ice cream with a dash of vodka straight from the tub and puts it back into the freezer, with her spoon *still* in it.
6. She thinks it's cool for her to have Facebook, Snapchat, Twitter and Instagram – please don't get me started.
7. She dresses like Miley Cyrus and says Chloë Grace Moretz is her spirit animal.
8. She wears T-shirts with slogans like 'Pink is a feminist issue' or 'Down for it.'
9. She tries to organise sleepovers for me with her friends' weirdo daughters in the hope that she can doss down with us and be 'one of the girls'.
10. She wants to give me a style makeover.

Stella

Tara loves my feature spread. I'm sure she does. I know she's really proud of her mummy for forging a stellar media career. I'm sure she thinks I take my inspiration from her wardrobe choices but the truth is, I wish Tara would be a little less Emily Brontë and Virginia Woolf in her attire. Would it hurt for her to buy a little Bardot top and show off those gorgeous little bony shoulders? If I had her tiny waist I would live in cut-off white shorts, frayed at the edges with a few strategically placed slashes. Still, she is learning from the best. Any day now, her love of fashion will kick in. It's just delayed, like when she didn't cut a tooth until she was thirteen-months-old. I thought she'd have gums forever.

I have to allow Tara to develop her own unique style. After all, we all went through the teen years fashion fails. I just wish she would take a little guidance from me, after all, I am in the fashion industry. She is privileged to have me by her side to oversee her shopping choices.

It isn't easy being a lone parent. Everyone says so. I have the hardest job on earth bringing up my baby girl all on my own. And look at me. Hardworking, successful, glamorous even. Just like Madonna; doing it all solo. Setting such a good example to my daughter. She learns first-hand how hard it is to be woman of substance. A woman of goals and needs. If I want to purchase a new Coach or Kate Spade handbag, then I know that I need to check my bank balance and make sure that my overdraft and credit card are all in alignment. That is the responsible, grown-up thing to do.

Maybe I'll treat myself to a new bag. Yes, I deserve an award for getting through a hard week of working, commuting and parenting. Bravo me!

I cannot believe that Madonna is sixty. How did that happen? One minute she's wearing a Gaultier cone bra and the next she is eligible for her bus pass. Along the way she taught us how to party, how to pray and how to be a badass woman while making no apologies. I must do a feature looking at how Madonna's fashion choices have influenced us over the decades. The Pope's visit to Ireland could tie in nicely. After all, nobody wears rosary beads quite like Madonna.

Want list:

- An ankle-length pleated skirt to be wore with flats, preferably plimsolls.
- A pug. They are all the rage. I could call it Tiffany or Ivy and take it to the office with me. Tara's cat may not

approve but they could end up devoted to each other. The Instagram possibilities are endless.

- A Jackie O style head scarf for the transitional weather we are having.
- Some cacti and succulents to create a green zone in the kitchen. It would look great as a back drop for Instagram posts.
- A hobby or a man. Or both.

Chapter 3

Do I really want to wear that?

Tara
Friday 9.12pm

Food eaten: not nearly enough.

> *Your presence is requested at the party of the year.*
> Heart *invites you to star at our soiree,*
> *12th May 2008 7pm for 8pm*
> *Henshaw's, Maiden Stone Square, Dublin*
> *Dress code: whatever goes*
> *RSVP juno@heartpublications.com*

The commuting part-time mother has returned. She swans in to the kitchen and swoops down on me for a kiss. Her Jo Malone perfume is cloying but I return her hug, in a bid to satisfy her maternal neediness and try to go back to my homework. Not a chance, she's going to hang around and look for some sort of *connection*. Often the conversation begins with my day at school and ends with her telling me every detail of her day. She looks at me expectantly. I can't think what it is she's waiting to hear and then she prompts me, 'Well, darling, tell me honestly – what did you think of the feature?'

I look at her childlike eager, expectant face and can't find it in me to burst her bubble of happiness and total self-involvement. You see, that's how nice I am really.

'Sure, it's great.' It's all I can manage without choking on my words.

'Really? You loved it? Oh, I'm thrilled. It's racing off the shelves as we speak. Can you believe it? In this internet dependent world, magazines are practically *dying* and yet my feature is a hit! Jago has just WhatsApped me to say Perpetua is expecting it to be their highest selling issue *ever*.' Stella is practically dancing around our slick grey and indigo kitchen, throwing chopped peppers and radishes into the huge bowl of salad leaves. She sets a bottle of balsamic vinegar on the table and arranges cutlery next to the slate place mats.

'Tara, what are you wearing? Didn't I buy you that, like, *two seasons* ago?'

I look down at the oversized T-shirt with a print of feathers across it and shrug.

'Darling, you really must try harder. You should ask yourself every morning, do I really want to wear that? And if you listen closely you will hear your inner fashionista whisper "no, put it back in the wardrobe". The key, darling, is to pay attention. Okay, sweetie?'

I sort of nod. No point in trying to explain that I was happy to put on the first thing that came to hand. This as a concept would be alien to Stella, sort of like explaining snow to a child brought up on the desert plains.

A jug of iced water with three slices of lemon floating on top is added to the table and with a flourish of the salad servers Stella announces in a sing-song voice, 'Dinner's ready.'

'What? This is it?' I ask, eyeing the bowl of salad with suspicion. It looks as if it has just been plucked from an allotment, wildlife and all for added protein.

'I know, darling, it seems a little light, but us girls have got to watch our calorie intake. Did you read the piece on BMIs written by our resident doctor, Jon?' Stella serves a generous portion of leaves onto my plate – as if she can make up for the lack of carbs and taste by being big on the garden arrangement. Oh yummy, lots of green stuff, that should fill me up. Not.

'It is just scandalous how many calories are hidden in food. It is so easy to pile on the pounds and now I'm in the public eye I really must be more responsible. My readers expect nothing else. I'm not saying I'm a role model per se, but young, impressionable girls are reading my work and nobody wants to see a roly-poly role model, do they?'

I promise you I am not making this up. She really thinks that she is someone of celebrity status or at least on her way to being there soon. I offer up a silent prayer that Madonna or Beyoncé declare that keto diet plans are over. Note to self: raid the fridge after dinner, before Kveta conducts her nightly swoop.

I try to tune Stella's buzzing high-pitched voice out. Since she has begun commuting to Dublin she has acquired a strange hybrid accent, sort of posh BT9 Belfast mingled with that plum-in-mouth voice of Keira Knightley.

Perhaps I could get one of those white-noise machines that would eliminate her simpering voice and give me peace to just think. Or ear defenders. They would be awesome.

Perhaps I am not being totally fair. She was on a high from the success of her first big magazine by-line. I can understand the sense of achievement from reaching her goal but really, does she think that writing fashion pieces for lobotomised teenagers is worthy of starvation? Or worse – starving her own daughter?

I could become anorexic and end up being force-fed with a rubber tube, lie languishing in a specialised hospital ward somewhere and then Stella would be sorry. Does she not know that teenage girls are impressionable? Maybe *Heart* magazine have yet to do a feature on anorexia. I may have to wait several issues before she has it from the authority of Dr Jon that children must be fed proper nourishing, fatty, tasty food.

I let her prattle on as I try to eat the shrubbery.

'Amazing bags, quirky little purses, fabulous suede fringed belts …' All she seems to care about is clothes and accessories. It is beyond me how anyone could find so many different ways to describe an outfit.

I zone back in, roused from my private imaginings of wasting away from lack of wholesome, filling food when I hear the terrifying words: launch party. At first, I thought I was having some sort of calorie withdrawal delirium episode, like Hurley in *Lost*. Do you remember *Lost*? Stella was obsessed with it for the first two episodes. She can't possibly expect me to tag along to some fashion magazine gathering, could she?

'You'll love it, honey. We can do a weekend trip and you'll get to see the apartment. It's très chic. Very *Sex in the City*. My own little pied à terre. You can meet all the gang. Jago, my assistant, is super cool, gay as a disco ball and has impeccable taste. Casey will be there too. She's the new teen agony aunt, you really must meet her – she's only twenty, can you believe it, and working for *Heart*?'

I let my fork clatter to the floor, anything to break my mother's mad rambling.

Gasping for air and grasping for a plausible excuse, I say, 'Mum, I can't go to a launch party in Dublin. I have exams coming up, projects to finish, you know how it is.' Hot tears of panic prick my eyes.

'Oh, baby, don't worry. I know you are fretting about not having anything suitable to wear but I will take you shopping. We can have a lovely girls' day out in Victoria Square trying on all the cute little frocks in Karen Millen and Ted Baker.' Could this woman be serious? Did she think my only concern was not having a stupid bloody dress to wear to her stupid bloody launch party?!

It is too much to bear. Not only would I have to witness my mother networking, in other words flirting, but I would be expected to be *entertaining*. Now I am not boasting when I say I have many talents – drawing, writing, consuming whole chocolate cakes in one sitting, but being entertaining is not one of them. I would never in a million years consider myself entertaining – you know, the sort of person who can *mingle*. It isn't that I'm shy as such; I have just never known what to say to inane air heads with skirts barely covering their arses. When I'm thrown into uncomfortable social situations

I always have an urge to burp or fart. I end up spending the entire conversation nodding, with my mouth shut and my buttocks firmly clenched for fear of letting myself down.

I eat the salad, resolving to demolish the remainder of the cheesecake in our oversized, under-stuffed American-style fridge afterwards, providing Kveta our Croatian au pair doesn't beat me to it.

I could beg Kveta to come up with some sort of plan to save me from the launch party. Perhaps Kveta will say that I couldn't possibly miss a weekend of study time. We could pretend to have a study rota that had to be adhered to. Stella hasn't got a clue about exam timetables or study rotas, never mind what goes on in school – it's as if she never went to school, that she was born writing drivel for brain-numb nutters – and she is terrified of Kveta so it might just work.

It would be torture beyond bearing – a shopping expedition; a weekend in Dublin sightseeing with my mother's undivided attention. How could I possibly survive? I must be being punished for misdemeanours in a past life. I just hope they were worth it.

Stella

She hovers around like an annoying little mosquito. I'm the worst mother ever but at least I know it. It's hardly my fault I was genetically programmed to be career driven and creative. Motherhood simply wasn't going to sustain me. My soul depends on being stimulated by fun, interesting people, not a whining, Gothic-styled daughter who could give Miss Havisham a run for her money in her fashion choices, determined to make me feel insecure every time I open my mouth.

Her head swivels round to watch me, making sure I'm not on my phone. For some reason, she has declared the dinner table to be a phone-free zone. We're supposed to 'converse about our day', but how am I meant to remember what my day consisted of if I can't access my Twitter feed or Instagram posts? She tuts as I photograph the salad bowl. The problem is, Tara doesn't understand how social media works. She still thinks it's for making friends, but at my level of interaction it is all about branding. With the number of followers I have, I am a legitimate influencer and that brings with it responsibilities to post important photographs of things like my dinner. People are interested. They truly are.

One cute pic of me eating a lettuce leaf taco could get me hundreds of likes. Besides it's fun to arrange a pretty table, set with quirky crockery and stylish glassware. Tara will thank me when she's older and has grown more appreciative of the little things in life.

Tara
11.45pm.

Can't sleep. I cannot, I will not, go to the stupid launch party for my mother's freaking magazine. Why can't she understand that I am not interested in fashion or make-up or sparkly, shiny things like she is? How is a handbag made of lizard skin and injected with Botox to make it soft worthy of conversation in the same way someone would discuss a painting by Degas, Brexit, Donald Trump's twitter habits or imminent ecological disaster?

Bad enough that she dragged me with her to every job she ever had until I was old enough to take a stand and say, 'no more'. Now she just jumps on the early train to Dublin most Mondays returning on Thursday evening, leaving me in the capable but oh-so-not-interested hands of Kveta. Then when she has work days in Belfast she is in the office until seven, flies in to change her outfit and handbag before leaving to go to some 'work' related do.

Basically, I live alone for most of the week with my au pair on hand to dole out money, food, and car lifts. My life sucks.

Matt says 'lucky me' but what does he know? He has a normal family and he's male – he knows nothing! I'm going to blog about it.

Lonely Girl Blog

Mothers should:

1. Cook proper family food, roast dinners with crispy goose-fat roasted potatoes, fluffy mash, flavoursome chicken slathered in gravy with peas, parsnips and turnip on the side. They should tell you they want to see a shiny plate because you are a growing girl and moan if you don't ask for seconds.
2. Not count calories, talk about BMIs or encourage their daughter to limit their carbohydrate intake. See above; I am a growing girl.
3. Speak in a normal Belfast accent, use colloquialisms like 'sweet Mary Jane' when needing a swear word, 'wee pet' as a term of endearment or 'poke' for ice-cream cone. Wear clothes from Hobbs, Phase Eight, Marks and Spencer's, Dunnes and Boden. Do not display excess flesh, EVER! Hot pants, boob tubes, Bardot tops and short kilts with knee-high socks are NEVER appropriate, especially not to school functions.
4. Not watch *Pretty Little Liars* or *Riverdale* or play Kings of Leon in the car at full volume or say that Lady Gaga is a scream.
5. Clean the house and not wait until it looks like a tip before calling in specialist cleaners who are really pest controllers in disguise, so that the neighbours do not discover you have mice living in the cupboard under the sink.
6. Not treat hired help or au pairs as slaves.
7. Avoid texting or using an iPhone at the dinner table.
8. Never have a mobile phone ringtone which is in the current charts, especially not an Avicii track. Why can't a simple *trill trill* sound do?
9. Never borrow their daughter's clothes, especially underwear.
10. Never suggest that their daughter borrow their clothes.

11.   Never suggest that the daughter calls her by her first name in public.
12.   Work nine to five in an office doing something vague like marketing, human resources or finance and talk about needing to go part-time and have flexi-time to create a better family/work balance.
13.   Avoid at all costs saying 'what's the craic?'; writing CBA, LOL, OMG, or WDF in any format; or thinking that it is acceptable to write notes to your teacher in text speak.
14.   Be married, preferably to their offspring's father.

I wonder would Nigella Lawson adopt me or Holly Willoughby – she looks like a proper mummy, all squidgy and soft with no hard angles.

Chapter 4

Candyfloss lip-gloss and Kveta, the au pair, in hiding

Saturday 9.06pm

Food consumed: French toast with cinnamon and maple syrup from the cute café on Stranmillis Road (Stella likes us to do breakfast out on the weekend), one packet of Doritos, (Chilli flavour,) wholemeal bread roll with ham and cheese (I picked the olives out), one small tub of custard, one bowl of Weetos, and pasta with aubergines and pesto.

Lonely Girl Blog

Spent this evening putting up with Matt ogling at Jessica Bailey's Instagram photographs.

Jess has uploaded the photos from her birthday party sleepover and of course, Matt was mesmerised. The first one showed Jess puckering up to blow out a single sparkly candle on a swirly icing covered cake. Then there was the obligatory group shot of the girls all posing, but looking like they were caught off guard. It was the final one that did the damage. There was the pouting, blonde Jess posing with her fluffy slippers and wearing her 'I Love Avocado' pyjamas spread across a grey sheepskin rug cuddling her dog, causing Matt to lose the power of speech.

'Get a life, or better still get a girlfriend. I can't take any more of this mooning over Jess. What do you see in her anyway?' I threw my stuffed elephant at his head, before getting off my bed and leaning over his shoulder to get a better view of the photographs.

Jess has glossy, lemony coloured hair which is straightened and highlighted and styled in a different way every single time I see her. She looks like she smells of wildflower meadows and kittens. In the photo pouting on her Facebook page she has her hair pulled into a sleek side ponytail. It's designed to look relaxed and effortless, but I know from experience any arrangement of a side ponytail takes work and time.

Her lips are puckered up and smeared with candyfloss pink lip gloss and she has clear, peachy skin which I am sure has never even seen a hint of a pimple or a crater pore. I know it's silly to pretend that Jess Bailey isn't attractive, pretty even, but really, does Matt have to rub my nose in it? I normally don't worry too much that I am a freckly, pale, ridiculously tall thing. Looks don't concern me. I have higher aspirations than looking like a homogenised teen version of a Bratz doll.

'Sorry, look, I'm logging out. Now tell me again why a weekend in Dublin is a bad idea,' he said as he swivelled round on my desk chair to face me.

'Matt, you know why. Firstly, it's with my mother and secondly, it's to go to the launch party for her stupid magazine. Can you imagine me standing amongst all those vacant Irish models and pop star wannabes?' I am completely exasperated because he refuses to see how difficult this is for me.

Then he picked up *Heart* and began flicking through it. 'Some people don't know when they're born. You could meet someone famous, think of the cocktails and the goodie bag. They always give you a goodie bag at those things. Hey, if you get an iPhone X in it, can I have it?' Can you believe him?

'Don't be a twat – it isn't the Oscars,' I said, hoping my voice was scorn-pitch prefect.

Sometimes, I despair. Matt just doesn't get it. It would be all right for him to go to a party, any party. He would stand in a corner until someone interesting spotted him and then find he was suddenly at the centre of it all, without even *trying*. He has a way about him, an easy-going, laid-back vibe that people seem to pick up on as being nonchalant and cool without trying too hard. Nothing is more attractive than someone who seems to just not care. Maybe my problem is that I care *too* much. Every decision I make is over-thought and over-analysed.

I told him I wasn't going so he would have to do without his goodie bag, just before I heard the unmistakably click-clack of my mother's kitten heel mules on the stairs.

Stella stuck her head round the door. 'Hi, you two, hope I'm not interrupting.' She was smirking in her affected tone of the cool mum.

I fired her what I hope was a withering look; I have given up trying to make Stella believe that Matt is not my boyfriend but I will not tolerate her insinuations. For pity's sake, if he was my boyfriend then technically we shouldn't be hanging out in my bedroom. I have pointed this out to Stella and she called me a prude.

'I'm just nipping into town to meet up with some people from the Belfast office. Kveta is in her room if you need anything. Don't wait up.' She blew me a kiss and departed, her heels beating out their clickety clack rhythm on the staircase.

'God, I wish my mum would leave me with a free house.' Matt sighed. 'You never use it to your advantage. We could be having a party. We could invite everyone from our year over and your mum would probably be really cool about it.'

As if. My mother would demand to be in the middle of it all, setting up beer pong tables and pass the Dorito competitions.

'It isn't exactly a free house. Kveta is lurking in her room,' I told him. He knows fine well that Kveta is always there, but he likes to pretend that I can come and go as I like.

'Does she ever come out?' Matt asked, doing that weird thing with his eyebrow where he arches it in a certain direction.

'Don't be so mean. She's just quiet. And withdrawn. And anti-social. And probably on a spectrum of some sort that hasn't been given a name yet.'

'Strange, more like she's a sad randomer. Kveta no-mates. Does she still not eat with you or your mum?'

'No, she prefers to eat in her own room when Stella is home, but she does eat with me during the week,' I said, feeling a tad defensive. After all, Kveta made my life easier.

To fill you in: Kveta arrived eight months ago. Stella found her on a private staff website called Staff of Kingsbridge. Their usual listings involve private chefs for yachting, sole charge nannies with degrees in child psychology and butlers, described as exceptional in their discretion. Kveta was found on a sister company website called Extra Help, and was advertised as a mother's help for older off-spring.

Stella likes the idea of having staff around the house. She has notions. Kveta said in her interview that she wanted to live in Belfast because it is the homeland of Westeros. A *Game of Thrones* fan who speaks of Jon Snow as if he is a God. I think she had planned on getting extras work on the programme but as far as I know she hasn't succeeded. On gaining the job as our live in au pair, and discovering she had Netflix and Sky TV in her bedroom, she created herself a cosy den and rarely appears when Stella is at home, unless summoned for instructions. She nearly always wears purple or black and sort of lumbers when she walks, doesn't speak unless she has to and has a strange sleeping pattern.

'She's a weirdo,' said Matt.

I shrugged. Kveta doesn't bother me so the arrangement suits us both. We have an understanding: I know where she is if I need her and I don't bother her if I don't. I quite like Kveta and her air of uninterest in the world. She looks world-weary as if she has seen it all and done it all before and is just marking time, even though she is only twenty-one. Or so she said on her online au pair profile. The only remarkable thing about her is her black-blue hair which hangs like a sheet of raven feathers down her back.

Matt's mobile wolf-whistled its ringtone. He tapped it open and read the text message.

'Gotta go. Late for training,' he said, bouncing up from the bed like he had just been ejected.

'But it's pouring down and it's nearly half past eight,' I said, certain Matt does not have Gaelic football training on Saturday nights.

'We're inside the hall, doing exercises for stamina. I'll see ya.' He loped across the room, his long legs covering the space in five footsteps, leaving me wondering where he was really rushing off to and sure that wherever it was, it had something to do with Jess Bailey.

Stella

Liv from the Belfast office has dragged me out for drinks. Sunday evenings are such a drag. All that dreaded 'work the next day' vibe needs to be medicated away. I'm not due in Dublin until Tuesday so what's the harm? It's a glorious night in Belfast. You'd almost think we were in a nice city, like Manchester or Edinburgh. We are gathered in the Harp Bar drinking bramble gin cocktails. We knock them back like they are homemade lemonades and the night feels sparkly and full of possibilities. Some little Irish dancing lad with blond curly hair and a cute smile, is putting on a display. They have a band playing diddly-dee music to accompany him, a bearded *bodhrán player*, a fiddler and a guitarist. It's all very 'Oirish'. A bit colloquial for my tastes but then I have lived all over. I am an international, cosmopolitan, citizen of the world, as Angelina Jolie would say. Still, I must admit, it's nice to be home. It's good for Tara to be here. She is better suited to Belfast life.

The party is spilling out to the street and someone grabs me by the arm and swings me round in a jig. Oh, what hilarity. I hope someone videos this for Facebook.

Liv whoops and sings along with 'Galway Girl' and we link arms and skip down the street before stopping to take a selfie. The street is so pretty, with bare light bulbs draped from wall to wall. We caption the post 'hump day drinks' thinking we are hilarious since it's a Sunday.

Then I have one of those moments. You know, that out-of-body feeling you get when you are out, surrounded by beautiful, happy people and suddenly you feel all alone? Sad even. You look down at your new shoes, twinkling in the moonlight and you don't feel a smidgen of joy?

Life's good. I have a job I love. I have a beautiful home. I have a wonderful daughter.

So why am I not happy?

I know! I need a tattoo. That would pick me up. Must research thoroughly though. Don't want to choose something that will look tarty in a few years. I can just imagine Tara giving me that soul-crushing look and telling me off; so it must be meaningful and significant. That is the responsible thing to do. Note to self: no mad, impetuous inkings.

***

One hundred and forty-seven likes and seven comments on Instagram. Must research hashtags to reach a wider audience. Not a bad night, all things considered.

Tara is looking at me with that face. The one that says she thinks I'm an inferior being. God, I hate that look. It reminds me so much of my mother.

'What?'

'You were out on a school night!'

'In case you hadn't realised I don't go to school.' I avoid making a face at her. That wouldn't be the motherly thing to do. Where's the au pair when you need her? Probably re-watching *Game of* bloody *Thrones* in her hideaway bedroom. Further note to self: do not make the bedroom so luxurious for the hired help. She really didn't need a double bed, an en-suite and a thirty-inch television.

'You know what I mean. A work night.'

'And your point is? I'm going to work from home this morning. Pyjamas are allowed. In fact, twenty per cent of millennials work from home in their pyjamas every day. If you read *Heart* magazine last month you would have come across that little nugget of information.'

Tara's pretty face scrunches up in disdain as she flounces off to catch her bus to school. Thank God she's gone. I don't think I could maintain the 'trying to appear not hung-over' disguise. Maybe I could go back to bed for an hour. Sleep through the hangover; I am sure I'll be much more productive when I wake up.

Tara
Lonely Girl Blog

11.08pm

Matt thinks I should wise up and get over myself. In other words, concentrate on the positives in my life instead of thinking of all the negatives. So here goes:

1. I live in a three-storey house overlooking a lush green square surrounded by copper beech trees.
2. My violet painted bedroom is large, with built in wardrobes, a well-stocked book case and a deep bay window seat on which I can curl up and read.
3. I have a fat, smoky grey cat called Cassius who thinks he owns the window seat in my bedroom.
4. I live in a relatively peaceful Belfast (one-off random shootings and recreational riots don't count when everyone else grew up with regular riots, bombs and murders).
5. I have good health, enough money, freedom and an education, which is more than half the world. Think of Malala.

There, that's it. Satisfied? I am spoilt, self-centred and too introspective, but hey, as a teenager that's practically my job description.

Chapter 5

The devious arts of being a woman

Stella

The problem with working in an office is that you are expected to turn up every day, even on days when you don't really have much work to do. I suppose I can surf through Net-a-Porter and Pinterest as research. It's good to be aware of the trends before they hit mainstream. I'm supposed to be a trendsetter after all. It's a little-known fact that it was me who instigated the avocado on rye toast craze. Though I am not responsible for the unicorns or cold-brew coffees. Definitely not.

I must remember to call Tara before she starts her homework. Last time I called in the middle of her study time she gave me a lecture on the need to respect her boundaries of no calls during school time. God, when I was at school I'd have loved someone ringing me for a bit of distraction. Though in my day we didn't have mobile phones. Sometimes I wonder where I got that girl from. Maybe they mixed her up in the maternity ward and I have been bringing up the spawn of two geeky scientists. She could be the love child of Stephen Hawking and Malala. So intelligent and earnest. Jesus wept.

To do list:

- I've three hundred words to write on athletic wear
- Order some groceries from Tesco
- Tell the Wildling au pair to pick up dry cleaning
- Call Tara

- Water the orchid in my Dublin apartment
- Book bikini wax (ask Tara if she would like me to book her in as well).

Right time to write some amazing copy. Here goes.

Come in close. I want to whisper something. Athleisure. You heard it here first. If you ask your mothers and grandmothers they may remember the great shell-suit catastrophe of the nineties. Leisure wear was constructed out of polyester in lurid colours of orange and turquoise. Scraped back ponytails and Nike high-tops completed the look. It was not attractive. It was not even practical – can you imagine running in a polyester suit? Fear not. This time round the designers have got it right. Trust me – this is a gift from above. Since we burnt our corsets and donned pantsuits, making comfort look stylish has been the holy grail of fashion. We are indebted to brands like Lululemon, Adidas, Nike, and Athleta for providing us with wearable, comfortable clothes. As usual we need to bow down to Beyoncé. She has given us permission to be comfortable and stylish.

It's such an honour to be working for *Heart* magazine. It really is.

'Stella, come play with me tonight, please.'

'Livvie, my darling, I have to be good this week. I'm on a detox.'

'Oh, I heard that if you alternate a detox day with an alcohol day it speeds up your metabolism.'

'Well, I suppose a little vodka cocktail can't hurt too much.'

'Yes, just don't eat any olives or peanuts and you'll still be on track.'

'Promise to keep me away from kebabs and burger vans afterwards?'

'Promise, hun.'

'You look gorgeous, darling. Quick, take a selfie with me.' Liv is wearing a gauzy floaty dress from Minx and I've a tight-fitted slate grey jumpsuit. We pose and take several pics and then delete most of them before posting the prettiest. Filter: Hudson.

The Dublin scene is hit and miss. Make a wrong turn and you find yourself in old man pubs with paintings of horses and dogs on the walls. We play it safe and stick to Grafton Street. There's a rumour that Ed Sheeran might drop by. He's supposed to be checking out a castle in Bray that he's buying as a holiday home or a wedding venue. Every time a ginger walks in the bar the crowd starts singing 'Castle on the Hill'. There's a lot of gingers in Ireland. That's the thing about the Southern Irish – they think they are hilarious and the truth is, they often are.

Tara
Saturday 7.30pm

Food demolished: one bowl of Weetabix with minging chocolate soy milk and sliced banana on top, cheese burger, spicy wedges, pint of Coke, banana and coconut cheesecake.

I wake to the sound of Stella singing an Ariana Grande song in the shower. For the love of all that is sane, please make it stop! I bury my head under my pillow, but Cassius knows I'm awake so he begins pawing at me to get up and feed him. I pick him up, my beautiful big purring fur ball, and give his gorgeous grey cat face a kiss and head downstairs. I'm still tired. Lately I haven't been getting enough sleep. Between fretting about my mum's stupid fashion party and being woken during the night by Kveta's strange rustling noises, I'm a walking zombie.

On the upside I have been using my late-night wakefulness to keep the blog updated and to create some rough sketches for a graphic novel idea which keeps bouncing around my head. I can't wait to start mapping out the story, but it's Saturday so the shopping day from hell looms.

'Morning, doll,' Stella calls as she sashays into the kitchen wearing nothing but her bra and knickers. I say knickers, but really they are little more than two triangles of lace held together by some elastic.

'Mum! Put some clothes on!' I avert my eyes as she skips into the utility room to find something to wear.

'Sweetie, there's only us girls around so don't be such a prude,' she retorts, pulling on her skin-tight jeggings. Of course Stella is chirpy and spritely, knowing that she has a day of retail worshipping planned.

We head off at ten and I gaze out of the car window watching Belfast blur past. Trees give way to restaurants, shops, pubs, all signs of a country out to enjoy itself. The remnants of riots and political graffiti may only be a few streets away, hidden out of sight, but on the surface Belfast is a city showing off, as if to say 'Ha, look at us!'

'Oh, come on! Can't you use your indicator,' Stella lambasts the car in front for overtaking her.

I barely raise an eyebrow; I am well used to Stella's road rage and her need to give a running commentary on everyone else's driving, like she is some sort of expert and the only driver worthy of being on the road.

I tried to come up with a good excuse to avoid the shopping trip but resistance was futile. Once Stella decides she needs to go shopping there is little to be done to stop her. 'Besides,' Stella had countered with a bit of a whiney tone, 'we need to spend some time together. I have hardly seen you all week.' As if it was my fault that she swans off to her other life leaving me home alone except for the reclusive Kveta and Cassius Claws.

But why does Stella think spending time together has to involve shopping for clothes? Answers on a postcard please. She works Monday to Thursday in Dublin, shows up home only to go rushing out to some art exhibition and spend whatever free time she does have at Total Bliss beauty salon waxing her legs, or what she calls her 'lady garden', and having her eyebrows reshaped. Besides, there are already countless outfits hanging unworn in my wardrobe. I hardly need new underwear let alone anything else. Stella has a habit of impulse buying and trying to assuage her guilty conscience for not being home enough by lavishing new clothes on me. She sees something and convinces herself that I'll love it and then buys it regardless of cost or the fact that I really couldn't care less.

'You do realise that all of these clothes you are planning on buying me have been manufactured in some sweatshop by children younger than me?' I say just to wind her up. Stella may be an avid consumer but she also has a conscience. She loves Bob Geldof and charity Twitter rants and ice bucket challenges.

'No, darling, we only buy quality. The more you spend the less likely it is to have been manufactured in challenging conditions,' she purrs. Nothing will knock her off her shopping mojo this morning.

When I dressed I pulled on my black Superdry T-shirt with a pair of scruffy faded jeans. No thought, no care, just simple. Why Stella has to invest so much thought, energy and money into clothes is beyond reason.

Lonely Girl Blog

Woke in a bad mood as shopping day from hell loomed. Of course, Stella was chirpy and spritely. Shopping is her hobby and she acts like it is a justifiable passion like painting or playing an instrument.

I can remember other similar outings when I was younger. I would be desperate to just hang out at the park, climbing trees or kicking a football, when all Stella could think of was to drag me around shops looking for the perfect outfit and accessories. I grew up in between racks of clothes, day dreaming that I could find my own personal Narnia on the other side.

Her voice was droning on. I wanted to block her out and just live in my head where I could map out entire universes in which my mother had no authority. I have a new character fully formed just waiting to come to life on a piece of paper. Shyla, a teenage survivor of an ecological disaster; she lives in a world which has been destroyed by greed, pollution and over-consumption. She is one of the Cave Dwellers, a race of people forced to live underground in caves to avoid the harsh rays of the sun, which is close to burning out.

At that moment, listening to Stella wittering on, I would have loved nothing more than to be let loose in my room with big blank A3-sized sheets of paper and a fresh box of charcoal to create preliminary sketches of Shyla and her Cave Dweller people. Unfortunately, Stella can never appreciate why I need to work on projects which are not designated homework. So, instead of spending a couple of hours sketching and outlining my Cave Dweller book, I was forced into bonding time with my mother. Punishment beyond.

'Right, here we are. Where shall we start?' Stella said, pulling in to a car parking space in the Victoria Centre. The ultra-modern underground car park has a weird sci-fi vibe.

I just shrugged; I wasn't going to enjoy this so I was determined not to make it easy for Stella. Why should I?

'Come on, honey. Let's start in House of Fraser and find some Ted Baker dresses.' Her face was shining with joy as if she has just suggested going ice-skating or go-kart racing. She was practically jumping up and down wagging her little Mulberry handbag tail in excitement.

I recognised the eager glint in Stella's eyes. She always acts like this when she's shopping; she goes into a trance-like state trying on clothes and swiping her credit card as if her life depends on it. She darts from rail to rail, fingering accessories, stroking fabrics. Pure, mind-numbing TORTURE.

The escalator carried us swiftly to the first floor. A mental calculation estimated that I had fifteen minutes to humour Stella before I could mosey on over to the Paperchase section. Once there I could lose myself in the beautiful notebooks and the gorgeous cards standing in sentinel-like rows. I could stroke the glossy wrapping paper, look at the novelty pencils and the cute little erasers shaped like Japanese dolls. But before I could negotiate some Paperchase time I would have to endure clothes shopping purgatory.

I trailed behind Stella, watching the robotic shop assistants primed and ready to pounce at the first sign of a cash transaction with their credit crisis worries wafting in the air, every-sale-counts desperation hanging over them.

'Watcha think?' asked Stella, holding up a pair of 7 For All Mankind impossibly skinny-legged faded-washed jeans with obligatory slashes. The price ticket dangled mockingly, screeching out £199.

'Too transitional?'

I might have agreed if I had known what transitional meant in connection with a pair of jeans.

'Mmm. How about these?' I pulled out a pair of dark coloured boot-legged jeans. Just the style a proper mother would choose. I could imagine Matt's mum teaming them with a little baby-blue cardi and a smart blouse, with a ruffled collar. Perhaps something out of Oliver Bonas, all prim and pretty and on the right side of quirky.

'Oh, darling, not exactly fashion forward, probably not even this season. Sweetie, you really should pay more attention.' As if paying attention to fashion dictators was mind improving.

Stella snapped through the rails, the hangers clacking in protest, discarding any she felt didn't deserve as much as a second look, let alone a try on.

'I knew I should have stocked up on jeans at Brown Thomas. Maybe we should both pop down to Dublin at the end of next week to have a bit of a splurge. I have been working so hard, after all, and you could do with a new style-over.' She gave me the tilt of the head look.

'What do you mean a new style-over? There's nothing wrong with how I look now,' I said huffily.

She turns the volume up a notch.

'Don't be so touchy. A new season brings new fashion opportunities. You don't know how lucky you are to have a mum in the fashion industry.' Can you believe her?

I rolled my eyes. Why did everyone think I was so lucky all of a sudden? What was lucky about being told by your own mother that you needed a new look? Surely my mother is supposed to love me regardless of sartorial differences.

Stella placed another pair of jeans back on the rack. 'Not what I'm looking for,' she said, and with the jeans dismissed as second rate to those selected by the buyers in Dublin, Stella led the way into the cosmetics department.

I eyed the endless counters of creams, foundations, blushers, eyeshadows, all competing in their garishness, with suspicion. There seemed to be a dictate that the make-up counter assistants had to wear as much of their products as possible.

I stopped at the Benefit counter. Names like Bad Gal, Dandelion face powder and Dear John for a face cream made me smile. The assistant pounced, obviously terrified of letting a potential customer pass by.

'Hi there, have you used our products before?' she squeaked in a high-pitched voice.

'Eh, no, I don't usually wear any make-up,' I replied, trying to politely move along before I was given the hard sell. The last thing I needed was to be transformed into a Barbie doll with shiny lip gloss and eyebrows like church windows to rival Jess Bailey's.

The sleek, ultra-polished assistant batted her long lashes and reached over to take my hand. 'Here, let me show you.' She dabbed a blob of honey-coloured foundation on the back of my hand and swiftly and expertly blended it into my skin.

'I thought so, you're a true redhead. This tone is best suited to your skin type.'

Before I knew what was happening Stella had subtly edged me onto the make-up chair and the assistant was applying cooling lotions to my skin. Her fingertips swept across my cheekbones, dabbing and smoothing the cream onto my skin. She gathered together three tiny pots of metallic eyeshadows in blue, silver and teal before telling me to close my eyes. With gentle sweeps of a brush, my eyelids were shimmering like the scales of a mermaid's tail. With a flourish, she slicked on some mascara and used an oversized make-up brush to add a touch of blusher before holding up a mirror for me to see the finished result.

It was like looking at a new, improved me. My eyebrows, normally so fair and faint, were clearly defined soft arches. My lashes, usually pale and pointless, suddenly gave my eyes an outline, accentuating them so that they no longer looked lost and piggy-like in my face. My freckles were blended into a peachy glow and my lips looked plumped, glossy and totally kissable. I am not exaggerating, this stuff worked wonders on me. Either that or it was some sort of illusionary mirror. I could see from Stella's face that she was delighted with the transformation.

I smiled like a gormless fool, amazed at my own reflection. 'Thanks, I had no idea make-up could make me look *better*,' I squeaked, in a voice that had strangely moved an octave higher to mimic the make-up counter girl in some sort of strange accommodation.

'Tricks of the trade. Don't worry, practice makes perfect. You'll soon work it out yourself.' Then she plied me with samples as Stella bought a face powder and lip gloss for me.

'Mum, I won't be able to do it myself,' I protested as we stood at the counter, 'I won't want to wear it.' I know if I try to do it myself I'll just end up looking like one of those elaborately made up lady boys from Thailand that I watched once on a documentary on the Discovery Channel.

Stella typed her pin number into the assistant's keypad to pay for our purchases, dismissing my protest. 'Shh, honey, maybe not yet but believe me, someday you'll appreciate the devious arts of being a woman.'

After a lunch of Caesar salad, minus the dressing, for Stella and a cheese burger with spicy wedges for me, we resumed 'the hunt', as we had begun referring to the shopping trip. Stella has spent her life looking for that elusive outfit, the most elegant black dress or the most perfect fitting jeans ever to be found. I had passed the point of complaining. It would be easier to go along for the ride and hope that Stella would find something she deemed worthy of buying sooner rather than later. It was better to humour her rather than fight against it.

Three shopping levels later, I stood in a changing room and sighed. The assistant was angling for a big sale and had cannily earmarked Stella as a woman with a big purse and little sense. She had piled our changing rooms with dress upon dress, top upon top, and a few pairs of straight-legged jeans in apple green, purple and orange. Much to my horror she had chosen two of everything, assuming that we wished to buy the same things, like some sort of weirdo mother–daughter double act.

Past experience had taught me that the only way for this misery to end was to go along with it and pick an outfit. I tried on a slinky silk jersey dress first. It had a cowl neckline, batwing sleeves and a ridiculously short hemline. The magenta colour clashed magnificently with my red hair, even if I do say so myself, but I figured if I had to try on something I might as well go for the most outlandish dress just to annoy Stella.

But, as I stepped out of the changing booth the assistant gasped, 'Oh my goodness. It's gorgeous – quick, Sammy, come over to see yer woman here in the French Connection dress.'

Another assistant wobbled over in a pair of platform shoes and murmured her agreement. 'Fabulous, you just need a pair of killer heels and you'd be a knockout.'

Stella popped out from her changing cubicle wearing the skinny green jeans.

'Tara, you look amazing, just like a model,' she squawked. I could feel a red heat flush up from my neck to my hairline. I knew I looked ridiculous. My long, pale legs looked even longer than usual because of the short hemline, and the colour was practically screaming '*clash*' at my hair.

'I just put it on for laugh, I hate it,' I said, glowering at them.

Stella put her hands on my shoulders and spoke to my reflection in the mirror. 'Oh, please, you have to agree the colour is perfect next to your skin tone. It's the ideal dress for the launch party. We'll take it.'

Now in my room with shopping bags scattered on the floor, I can at last stroke the suede cover of my newly purchased notebook. It feels weighty and significant as if anything written on the creamy white pages will be worthy and important. While the decorative paisley prints had caught my eye, it was the texture and smell of this leather-bound notebook which captured my heart. Never in a million years would my mother recognise the beauty of such an item. If it couldn't be worn as an accessory then it was hardly worth buying. But I can appreciate the potential of a blank notebook. It represents possibilities like an unformed idea just waiting to take shape and evolve across the pages of my new, thick, cream-paged notebook.

Perhaps Stella's stupid shopping trip wasn't so bad after all.

Chapter 6

Poets, Misprints and Tippex

Stella

I'm on a mission to bond with Tara. To this end I have researched cultural outings in Belfast. Once I clicked past the Twelfth of July celebrations, bonfires and Orange parades, I found a poetry evening being held in a little bookshop on Botanic Avenue. Poems, serious smart people, probably a little bit hipster, surrounded by books – Tara will love it, I'm sure.

We can wear matching black turtleneck jumpers, little straight-legged cigarette pants and kitten heels, and look all Audrey Hepburn. First, I must swot up on poetry. Someone is bound to ask me who my favourite poet is and I can hardly answer Seamus Heaney. Every bog cutter from here to Donegal would reply Heaney. No, I'll say Sylvia Plath. I'll declare that her work awakened the feminist in me. Must find my old glasses, the ones I ordered when geek chic was a thing. I hope they serve wine.

***

The first poet takes to the floor and clears his throat as the room falls quiet. He reads a poem about a river cutting through a mountain and uses words like 'shuck' and 'gorging'. He tells us that 'the wide lips of the river mouth are swelling', all of which makes me want to giggle. It's the seriousness of his expression. His weasel-like face contorts in earnestness as he reads, pronouncing each word like he has practised this for weeks, which I'm sure he has. I can't help thinking his poem is an expression of all his sexual desires neatly encapsulated into nine stanzas. Tara looks on, oblivious to my struggle to remain composed. Honestly, if I don't distract myself I'm going to have to pretend to sneeze to avoid the onset of the giggles. I don't think my pelvic floor can sustain this level of hold.

I'm saved by the end of the poem and the audience clapping in appreciation. I hope the other readings are less hysterical or I'm going to have to leave.

Tara
Lonely Girl Blog

Monday 9.45pm

Food consumed since dinner time: one slice of chocolate cake, one bowl of Rice Krispies, and a cup of herbal tea with a Jaffa Cake dunked in it for flavour.

Stella made me go to a poetry reading. Oh, my Lord. She thinks I'm a closet poetry geek. I thought it would be full of pretentious people mumbling about haiku and syntax, but they seemed strangely *normal*. Apart from the weirdo at the front with an oversized beard and Jesus sandals.

The readings were actually good. There was one poem about war that made me feel all the feels. The poet was from northern Syria and he spoke in such a calm, measured, quiet voice that it was hypnotic. Afterwards we all stood around looking at books and making polite conversation. I suppose it was one of the better nights out I've had with Stella.

General life update:

Fact: My life is freaking me out. My best friend Matt has taken to hanging around the Lisburn Road in the hope of bumping, and I mean literally, into Jessica Bailey. He is making do with fantasies of her finding him irresistible up-close and personal. Personally, I think the plan will backfire – if she gets too close she will see the acne craters and the boil currently shining on his forehead like a squat toad. But that's for him to work out for himself.

Fact: I was a misprint. According to a conversation I overhead between my mother and her cohort* (nice word ain't it?), who had drunk three cocktails each (I should know, I was the one ferrying the jug from the ice maker to the dining table), I was not intended to be.

Not that it would have taken a leap of imagination to work out that I was indeed a mistake, an accident, an unwanted pregnancy, but I had never really dwelled on it before, and so hearing it come direct from my mother's slurring mouth stung just a little. They sat in their 'lounge wear', as Maura calls their tracky bottoms, eating oily stuffed olives and chopped vegetables dipped in tiny pots of humus bought from the local deli, Arcadia. It was their weekly after-yoga catch up.

The conversation went something like this:

Mother: 'We all make little typos from time to time and all I'm saying is that sometimes a little Tippex is required to make your page virginal clean again.'

Elise: (gesticulating wildly with her glass) 'Stella, what are you saying?'

Mother: 'Just that if the same thing happened to my little typo I would offer her a bottle of Tippex.' She dipped a carrot stick in a green gungey-looking dip and popped it in her mouth, before snapping it in two between her recently whitened teeth.

Joni: 'I'm with you, Stella, sometimes mother knows best.'

Maura: 'How could you even go there! She's only fourteen. She won't be thinking of inking her page for at least another four years, yet.'

Mother: (still crunchy her carrot stick) 'That may well be, but we all know that times have changed.'

To which they all murmured assent and resumed drinking with conviction.

So there you have it: I am a blot on my mother's blank sheet of paper. A misprint to be eradicated, except somehow she had failed to be given a bottle of Tippex when she needed it.

*Cohort = the Coven, my mother's three friends, Elise, Maura and Joni. She has known them since her convent school days so they are all bound to each other by knowledge of their former style mistakes in the nineties. (This is my mother's excuse for still seeing them even though she feels she has moved on in life, i.e. has a better job than them, social life, and a lower BMI).

They are all variations on the same theme: desperately trying to hold on to how they looked and felt in their late teens and early twenties.

Note to future self: trying hard to look young when it is obvious that time is having the last laugh is so not a hot look.

They all like to shop in Top Shop and Zara and discover hip boutiques hidden in arcades. Then they display their latest acquisition with pride as if having won the competition because they have spun a fresh interpretation on something similar to what they already own. Make no mistake, it's all about competing with them. Even when it comes to their children. Being the oldest of the offspring I am somehow held up as a bad example; what not to do in child rearing.

I have heard plenty of stories from my childhood, recounted by a tipsy Stella, which highlight her bad parenting skills. Like the time I had chickenpox and she thought it was early onset acne. Or the impromptu holiday we went on, only to discover it was an 18 to 30 club week in Ibiza. Or the nativity play in which I was to play the Virgin Mary and Stella sent me dressed as the other Madonna for a hoot. (She exaggerates this totally. I had leg warmers under my blue tunic but that was her only tribute to her icon Madonna or, as she calls her, the real Queen.) The others would chortle and say something like, 'Oh, Stella, aren't you a scream. Thank God the poor child turned out all right.' I can tell they don't mean it. They don't think I turned out so great.

If she has a hangover in the morning I shall offer her some Tippex.

10.20pm

Phoned Matt and told him about my mother's copy book. He laughed and told me to store the knowledge away and use it for my benefit in time of need. Don't know what he thinks I could do with it. I can hardly blackmail my mother with the knowledge that she had an unwanted pregnancy when I am the product of that biological gestation. (Learnt that word in Biology today – Mr Gimpsey was wearing trousers which are about five centimetres too short and when he sits down I can see a glimpse of his spidery hairy shin. Nauseous making).

Spent free study period with Matt listing ways in which I can annoy my mother:

1. Piercings, nose, tongue or belly button – Matt's suggestion. Had to be dismissed since she has already had all of the above at some stage in her life, although she only wears earrings now. Plus, didn't tell him but I did once see the glimmer of a nipple ring when I walked into the bathroom without realising she was in the bath. Traumatised for weeks afterwards.
2. Pretend to have had underage sex. Matt suggested leaving a condom in my room for her to find but she would probably congratulate me on being responsible enough to use a 'safety bag against life' (her name for condoms).
3. Drugs and drink are options but too much of a wuss to try either.
4. Stage a coming out party and declare that I'm a lesbian. Viable option but she would delight in it and view it as a something to brag about to all her bisexual and gay friends.
5. Become a geek. Study so hard that I become a freak of knowledge and only watch Bill Oddie and David Attenborough wildlife documentaries for entertainment.

It appears that my mother is unshockable and beyond being freaked out. Psychologists say that all teenagers must rebel as a matter of course – something to do with surges of hormones, but my mother has denied me this mile stone. She has done it all.

Lonely Girl Blog

11.45pm

Logging on.

Hi, it's me, Belfast Girl.

Something's woken me. A strangle rustling sound and now I can't sleep. It's probably Cassius chasing a mouse but I'm fed up and feel sorry for myself.

Basically, I live alone for half of the week with the au pair on hand to dole out money, food, and car lifts.

My BMF (best male friend) says lucky me, but what does he know? He has a normal family and he's male – he knows nothing!

To prove to you how pathetic my mother is, read this; it's her to-do list which I found on the bathroom floor. She writes lists while she is on the toilet.

To Do List

- Check in with my 3,299 Twitter followers – my people need me.
- Hot yoga with goats download – fifteen minutes at least, need strong abs and defined glutes – not sure what glutes are but I want them. If it works for Gwyneth it will work for me.
- Update my Pinterest board. Need to focus on motivational mantras and create a virtual wardrobe so that I can have a reference point for every occasion this season.
- Sky Plus season three of *The Affair*.

- Pick up some nosh at the deli on the corner; craving their dried pears and walnuts. Mmm, and maybe some balsamic onion cheese. Just a sliver.
- Pick up dry-cleaning or at least text the Wildling au pair to pick it up.
- Pay au pair. Make sure she changes my bedclothes and stays home to meet the Tesco online lad. I don't want her missing him yet again.
- Write 500-word column on summer collections even though it is still ball-freezing April.
- Blag tickets to see the Killers. God, Brandon Flowers is so hot.
- Skype daughter.
- Maybe I should do a feature on peasant wear.
- Feature ideas: Strapline: *Back to the homestead. We take a look at what our grannies wore and see how you can inject a shot of peasant into your summertime wardrobe.* Time for a skinny latte and a fag, methinks.

Chapter 7

Tara

Attack of the festering spot
Saturday 8.45pm

Food scoffed: Ulster fry (eggs, bacon, sausage, potato bread, soda farl and beans) purchased from the dirty café on the corner of University Street, as Stella needed hangover food. Chinese takeaway – chicken fried rice and curry sauce, followed by cuppa soup – chicken and leek.

Lonely Girl Blog

Hung out with Matt all day. Even though it is Saturday, Stella has been otherwise occupied with a fashion shoot in the Glens of Antrim, of all places. They are doing a fairy themed shoot. All wispy fabric and elf ears.

Matt and I climbed on top of the wall surrounding Stranmillis College grounds, positioned ourselves right next to the adjacent five-foot-high railings where we could watch the comings and goings on the Stranmillis Road. Nearly fell off when Matt asked me to help him out with his skin problems.

'A makeover? Are you serious?' I spluttered, not even trying to hide my disdain. What was the world coming to when Matt was looking for skincare advice?

'Not a makeover, you twunt, I just need you to nick some stuff from your mum's bathroom to sort out this zit.' He pointed, completely unnecessarily, to the pulsating growth on his forehead.

It was so big and angry it should have had a computer game based on it –A*ttack of the Festering Spot.*

I considered it for a second, that boggy-looking growth, and in a moment of weakness felt sorry for him even though I know that his only desire to have clear skin is to impress Jessica Bailey. So I told him: 'Sure, come on, we've nothing better to do anyhow. I'll see what I can do.'

Stella's bathroom is an extension of her boudoir bedroom. Rococo-style mirrors and subtle lighting creates a girly setting of powder puffs and perfume. But beneath the fairy lights and the crystal bottles there is a laboratory of high science, for Stella takes beauty very seriously. What she doesn't have stocked behind the mirror-covered cupboards isn't worth buying (when Space NK sold out of that bee venom serum stuff Stella laughed – she already had a month's supply purchased in advance); besides, another perk of her job is that she gets to swap unwanted clothes and accessories with the beauty editor for all sorts of lotions and potions.

I am forever finding sample-sized pots of moisturisers and cleansers left on my bed all wrapped up in expensive-looking packaging, like little trinkets of love. If my mother can't look after me properly at least she can lavish me with cleansers and lip balm.

'Right, sit down,' I instructed, while I set about opening up the mirrored doors. Rows and rows of assorted bottles stood to attention making it look like a chemist's back room.

I looked at the spot in question. No doubt about it, it was worthy of a mention in *Weird and Wonderful Medical Discoveries*, so green and *alive* did it look.

'So is there a specific reason this needs dealing with or are you just beginning to show more interest in your personal hygiene?' I asked him.

He said, 'Could be a sign that I am maturing and taking an interest in how I look. It's sexist if you think only girls care about their appearance. I just think I wouldn't want to run into someone with this thing sticking out of my head.'

Sharon Dempsey

That someone would of course have blonde hair and pouty lips. I can imagine Jessica Bailey in all her loveliness being confronted with the lesion of doom. Perhaps it would boil up in a fit of pressure due to the intense passion lurking in Matt's bloodstream and erupt all over her powdery made-up face. The thought of it cheered me up.

I went back to the shelves of products - cleansers, exfoliating lotions, abrasive creams, moisturisers - they all looked so scientific. So gloriously toxic.

'Hold still.' I squeezed a generous dollop of yellow medicinal-looking cleansing lotion onto a pink cotton-wool ball and placed it firmly onto the mound.

'Ow! Be careful. It bloody well hurts,' he yelped like a baby. Honestly, men know nothing of what some women happily go through to look good.

'Oh, please, did no one ever tell you that you have to suffer for vanity – it's the rule. Why do you think models and actresses all look so miserable?' I wiped the gloopy lotion away to reveal a still angry hillock. 'We might need to be more proactive.'

'What's that supposed to mean?' asked a bewildered Matt.

'Steam, that's what. I'm sure there's a steam facial system in here somewhere.' I rummaged in the bottom of Stella's walk-in closet amongst shimmering fabrics and silky dresses.

I found it and carried in the oval-shaped appliance, which looked more suited to the kitchen than the bathroom.

'What are you planning to do with that contraption?'

'Steam the blighter, that's what.'

I plugged the facial machine in and added enough water to create a plume of steam when it heated up.

'Try this,' I said, slathering Matt's face with a blue-tinged cream which smelt foul and ever so venomous, kind of like Vicks Vaporub mingled with disinfectant. 'Now stick your face in there,' I said, forcing his head into the rubber-coated outline of the facial steam bath.

'It's hot,' Matt mumbled from beneath the steam.

'It's supposed to be. Stay still and let it soak into your pores.' I tried to sound like I knew what I was talking about.

'No, I can't stick it. It's burning.' Matt lifted his face up and to my horror the blue cream had began to bubble and spit.

'Get it off me, it's bloody burning,' he shouted.

I began splashing water onto his face to cool him off, all the while thinking *Bloody hell, what I have I done?*

I said, 'You're such a baby, Matt. You were supposed to let the vapours work for at least ten minutes.' But as I finished the sentence I saw that the places where the blue lotion had rubbed away had left exposed raw welts of scalded tissue, all over his face.

'Oh. Oh. Oh …' It was all I could manage before yelling for Kveta. It looked like his skin had bubbled up into sweltering blisters.

'What? What is it?' asked Matt, pushing by me to look in the mirror.

'You've marked me for life, you stupid cow! You dickhead! You melter!' Matt peered at his reflection, as if he could stare the blisters away while running out of insults.

'Does it hurt?' I asked tentatively, trying to sound concerned.

'What do you think?' he said, just as Kveta came to the rescue.

'You burn your skin with lotion? I think you need to see a doctor, Matt,' she said as she dabbed aloe vera onto his skin. 'I don't want to risk making it worse. You should call your mother.'

'How do I explain this at school?' he said wearily.

'Don't worry, we'll think of something,' I said, trying to suppress a giggle. As contrite as I was to see Matt's sorry, sore face I couldn't help thinking how ridiculous the whole episode was. His vanity had been his downfall and Jessica Bailey would never know it had all been for her precious benefit.

11.12pm

Can't sleep. Again. Thought I would think of nice things to lull me into slumber.

Things I like:

1. Sparkly pens in pretty colours like bubblegum pink and lime green.
2. The internet and the random things you come across, like did you know that the little bubble bits on seaweed are called air bladders?
3. Boys who are cool and don't go all gaga over some stupid, brain-dead, beautiful girl. Why are looks so important anyway?
4. Swirly covered notebooks with lovely thick creamy pages.
5. My bed, especially when the sheets are freshly laundered. Thank you, Kveta.
6. Cassius, my cat. He is the most adorable hair ball ever.
7. Crepes with Nutella from Maud's.
8. Northern Irish beaches. They are never sunny, so my skin doesn't fry and they are almost always empty.
9. Reading a dictionary for the fun of finding new words.
10. Writing stuff down that I have made up.

Stella

I must bag myself some new items from the Wolf and Badger website. There's a silk emerald green jumpsuit with a gold coloured belt that would look divine on me. I could dress it up with some beaten copper jewellery for evening wear. I wonder if Tara would approve?

Christ, the thought of wearing something deemed inappropriate with those eyes giving me the evil glare. Shudder. She gives me flashbacks to my mother.

Calm, Stella. The mother-from-hell cannot have power over you now. You are a grown woman. You have travelled the world independently. You have birthed another human being. You have a mortgage and a Wildling au pair. You do yoga and can stimulate certain nether regions just by thinking of a shirtless Tom Hardy and a windswept Aidan Turner.

I know I can't avoid her forever. The Mother. Oh, the angst of returning home. I feel like I am seventeen again and need to seek out her approval, which was never forthcoming.

She wants to see Tara. I know I should do the right thing, but I'm too tired to deal with the emotional fallout. What would Beyoncé do in this situation? She'd write a song I suppose. Just like Taylor, have a rough patch, pour it into lyrics and make a million squid.

It's a pity I'm not musical. Perhaps I should write a poem about it all?

Lonely Girl blog

When I arrived from London, fresh faced and world-weary, I had to undertake an examination. Not just any exam but the eleven-plus equivalent. This one-hour test paper decided my educational fate. If I passed I was able to attend one of the many grammar schools filled with smart, middle-class students. If I failed I would be left with a choice of one comprehensive or several secondary schools with low achievement and lower expectations. Thankfully I passed.

Now this particular exam is such a big deal in NI; if you don't pass you are deemed a failure for life. You'll end up being something like a sausage packer in a meat factory when really you were supposed to be surgeon or a marine biologist or find a cure for cancer, but because you flunk a stupid test on one particular day of your impossibly short childhood, your life is deemed over.

According to Matt, in NI from the age of eight to eleven the only thing parents discuss is the eleven-plus. It has been such a problem here that the Assembly (not school assembly but the government assembly, though most of the time they do behave like they are in the playground) have outlawed the eleven-plus. This has been big news. But the teachers and parents love the power of the exam so much that they have decided to keep the eleven-plus going in an *unofficial* capacity. So now instead of doing one unified exam for everyone, they have two different systems, depending on whether you go to a Catholic school or a Protestant school. (I don't know what the Jews, Muslims or Hebrews do, never mind Humanists or Atheists – though Matt says there are no atheists in NI.) And instead of just one exam taken over two separate days, now you may have three or four exams depending on which schools you want to try out for.

Just thought I would tell you about it in case you wanted to move here and thought the schools were the same as in England. Oh, and by the way, schools here also work on a Catholic/Protestant agenda. You attend one or the other with the odd exceptional mixed school. And they wonder why they have problems!

Chapter 8

Blue tit bra nests and religious gnomes

Saturday 6.06pm

Food consumed: two rounds of toast, one banana, one apple, one bowl of strawberries, one mango, one bowl of Weetos, Subway meatball sandwich, one hotdog, one cup of herbal tea with chocolate fingers to stir it.

I have a job. Did you hear me? A job. An actual working-for-money job. Okay, so I spent most of the day shovelling dog poo and wiping drool off my sleeve, but at least I am doing something independent of my mother and school. Yee haw!

So Nora, my boss, is a bit of a first-class weirdo. She is a woman of few words and has a bit of a sour cat/doggy odour problem, but then so would I if I shared my house with twelve dogs, sixteen cats, two parrots, twelve budgies and thirteen canaries. I have probably left out a few others: I thought I saw a squirrel in the house but I could have been wrong – it is very dark. She also keeps bats and hedgehogs and there is an injured fox, but I haven't been allowed to see her yet. Nora said she was too traumatised to be 'interfered' with. She had been hit by a car and left for dead on the side of a dual carriageway and someone who knew about Nora's shelter took pity on her and called her. Oh, and there is a duck called Gypsy who marches up and down the garden like she is patrolling the place.

She also has a little black poodle called Skipper, who only has three legs. He is her pet and is *never to be rehomed*. She warned me twice that I was to never give him away. He follows Nora everywhere and whimpers like a little lamb instead of barking when he wants out.

I arrived at the shelter, which is actually just a large house, at the prearranged time of 9.30am

It looked sort of run down and dishevelled. The type of house you know an old person lives in.

I pushed back the trailing greenery to make my way up the overgrown path, which was covered in a carpet of slippery green moss. Brambles and tall, pink and lilac lupins jostled for position, as if to have a good look at me. The front door, which was painted a sombre dark blue, was crackled and peeling and needed a coat of paint. The windows, inky dark and empty of curtains or any sort of blinds, looked nakedly onto the garden. I was a bit spooked to tell the truth. The overall impression was that this house belonged in an episode of *Scooby Doo*, or *Britain's Most Haunted*.

I jangled the old brass bell, half expecting the rusting chain to fall off in my hand. It chimed out, summoning someone from the depths of the house. Dogs yelped from the back of the house and I could definitely hear a bird squawking loudly.

'Yes?' a voice seemingly disembodied called out from behind the door.

I said, 'Eh, I'm Tara. My mum said she spoke to you about a part-time job helping out with the animals.'

'Round the back,' came the gruff reply.

I stood forlornly on the stone step. It wasn't a promising start to my new job. Ever since Stella had suggested that I start work at the St Francis of Assisi Animal Sanctuary I had been buzzing with happiness. For the first time ever, it felt like Stella was on my wavelength and was accepting me for who I am, not trying to mould me into a plastic fantastic dolly girl, all make-up and ironed-out hair.

The thing is, I have always loved animals. Every animal book ever written has been devoured by me. All those with the simpering puppies and kittens on the covers have been lined up on my bookshelves forever. My all-time favourite book is *My Family and Other Animals* by Gerard Durrell. It is a bit hard, but, give it a go. I promise you it is worth the read. I always go back to it and love the descriptions of Corfu, his mad family and the assorted animals and insects he rescues and looks after.

I am currently into the James Herriot books too, even though they are a bit old-fashioned. If I wasn't set on being a graphic novelist I would happily be a vet or marry a farmer.

I have been pleading with Stella all my life to have a puppy, a rabbit, a terrapin, anything that moved and breathed. Something to care for and love, but Stella always balked at the idea. 'They're dirty, they chew, they smell, no way.' She eventually gave in and let me have Cassius when we moved here, but I think it had more to do with the mouse droppings under the sink cupboard than any wish to make me happy.

Granted our flat in London wasn't ideal, but when we moved to Belfast I held out a smidgen of hope that Stella would see the benefits of a having a slobbery big Labrador or a cute little kitten.

When Cassius arrived, a tiny bundle of mousy, brownish-grey fluff wrapped in a soft pink baby blanket, I swear my heart missed a beat. I could hardly believe that Stella had acquiesced, but the burden of guilt of uprooting me from my few friends and school in London to live in Belfast had swayed the decision.

Of course, I never let on that I wasn't so sorry to see the back of London anyhow. I didn't really have any proper friends to miss, not that I would ever tell Stella that.

So I am revelling in the knowledge that parental guilt can get you what you want. Stella has been working non-stop and socialising every bit as hard, resulting in very little daughter and mommy time. We have been virtual relatives with FaceTime, texting and emails providing our regular contact. As a make-it-up-to-me gesture, Stella arranged for me to work weekends and holidays at the animal shelter.

When I first voiced the idea of getting a part-time job, Stella had suggested modelling work. I had almost retched at the idea. Modelling, or in other words, standing like an inane mannequin, makes me dizzy and nauseous. Animated coat hangers with heads too big for their bodies is how I view most models. I have to admit that Matt is right about Kate Moss being a bit different and attractive in an older woman sort of way, but except for Kate and maybe Bella Hadid and Daisy Lowe they all seem like overpaid, ego-inflated morons. Not that anyone in their right mind would have let my face grace their books anyhow.

But then, one day out of the blue, Stella mentioned St Francis's shelter. She had run into the owner and they needed someone to help cover weekend shifts, mucking out, dog walking, that sort of thing. It sounded too perfect for words. Just like a Gerard Durrell book. I could wear what I liked and just hang out with abandoned dogs and scruffy cats. Almost too good to be true.

I hadn't counted on the other wildlife – Nora.

Anyway, back to today:

I made my way around the back of the house, clambered over nettles and a discarded tyre and almost jumped out of my skin when I came face to face with the crone-like appearance of my new boss. If the Lyric theatre is staging Macbeth they would do well to call on Nora to be one of the witches. Good manners all but prevented me from yelping and jumping backwards, for Nora is unkempt to say the least. Her tawny hair is streaked with grey and shot out in a wild halo of frizzy curls like an electrocuted cartoon character. Her skin is as lined and wrinkled as one of Stella's lizard skin handbags and her clothes are a motley assortment that have the air of charity shop rejects. I took in every detail from the brown woollen scarf entwined around her neck and the long, hole-infested cardigan, which could have been a pea green colour many years before, but now could only be described as sludge. On her feet she wears the biggest sized pair of green wellies I have ever seen.

'I'm Tara, I've come about the job?'

'Right, over there, start cleaning out that cage.' She pointed with a gnarled ochre-coloured finger towards a series of hutches and cages stacked along one side of the long, walled garden. So, no small talk. Fine, I thought, best get on with the job.

I looked around to see what I was meant to be cleaning with and found a shed stacked with brushes, shovels, a wheelbarrow and accoutrements.

An hour had passed before Nora showed up again.

'Good, you can start in the kitchen next. The dogs will be wanting fed.'

All thoughts of playing with cute puppies and fluffy kittens were dispelled as I made my way into the grotty kitchen to start doling out smelly dog food.

From what I can gather, Nora spends some time every day praying and lighting candles to St Francis to help heal the sick animals. I tried not to laugh when she told me to genuflect before St Francis's statue but a guffaw did almost escape my lips as I pursed them closed tight, for fear of insulting or offending her. Still, each to their own as my mum would say. I sort of did a little curtsy and bowed my head like I had seen at school Mass, at which Nora nodded her head in approval.

There is a washing line strung across the back yard – a sort of courtyard, only not so grand – and on the washing line hangs an old greying bra, pegged at either end so that the huge cups are like two hammocks. Now get this – inside one of the hammock cups is a nest of a family of blue tits! Hilarious!

They are burrowed far down in amongst twigs and scraps of moss and leaves, but every now and then I see the mother dart out to find some food for her babies. It's like a blue tit bra hotel.

At the bottom of her wild, overgrown garden she has a rockery which is kept free from weeds and has little shrubs and heathers growing. Among all the plants and the assorted shaped rocks there is a statue of Mary. She stands nearly a metre tall, her head tilted to one side with that quiet smile she always has in pictures, and the powder blue shawl on her head, the palms of her hands turned upward as if to welcome you to this little piece of paradise at the bottom of Nora's garden. Mary, the mother of Jesus, standing like a religious gnome. So not only is Nora, my new boss, rude, smelly, and totally disorganised, but she is also a religious fanatic.

Still, all in all a good day.

Things I learnt today:

1. St Francis is the patron saint of animals, the environment, and Italy.
2. He wanted to be a writer, specifically of French poetry, but his father had other ideas and made him work in the family business of selling cloth.
3. Although he was a wild teenager, he had a spiritual crisis after an illness and found his true calling.

A mysterious note and dog walking with Ollie
Monday 7.03pm

Food digested: one bowl of Weetabix with raisins, one squishy pear, one packet of cheese and onion crisps, one BLT sandwich, one of Kveta's indistinguishable dishes of goo, half packet of chocolate digestive biscuits, can of Diet Pepsi, toast with peanut butter and chocolate buttons on top. Delish.

Lonely Girl Blog

Matt has got a detention. Miss Gracey caught him trying to copy Jessica Bailey's physics test paper. I know different; the sicko was just trying to cop a look at her breasts.

He is still huffing over the Mount Vesuvius incident. Apparently, the blue gloop was a chemical face peel which reacted with the cleanser and was activated by the heat of the steam. His mother said he was lucky not have serious facial burns. The doctor said he would heal eventually and that he shouldn't scar, but Matt has taken it all rather personally. He is convinced that I deliberately tried to scald his face because I want to sabotage his chances with Jessica Bailey. *As if.* Firstly, what do I care if he manages to go out with her and secondly, he is delusional.

It. Is. Not. Going. To. Happen. Ever.

Rae phoned Stella to complain. She said Stella was being 'most irresponsible in allowing us to play together unsupervised'. What planet is she on? Stella practically laughed in her face except she was on the telephone, so it should be that she practically laughed in her ear. Poor Rae doesn't know how to handle Stella.

Still, if Matt is otherwise occupied I can get on with sketching. I have the first five chapters of the Cave Dwellers mapped out – in my head. The tricky part is getting it out of my head and onto paper. I have set myself a week by week deadline, all worked out on a spreadsheet. We have covered basic spreadsheets in information technology class. By my reckoning if I meet each weekly deadline of 3,025 words by July, I will have finished my first graphic novel. Obviously I need to factor in drawing time and time off for studying and any unforeseen happenings, but at least it has made the novel seem more real. I have begun doing my research for agents and publishers. This has taken up quite a bit of my writing time so I shall have to account for a shortfall of 2,699 words for this week. Maybe I should reassess my word count expectations. Don't want to get off to a poor start.

Doing homework tonight – maths (experimental probability: 'The probability of obtaining a 6 when I throw a die is $1/6$ – so if I throw the die 6 times I should get exactly 1×6.' In theory this statement is true, but in practice it is unlikely to be the case. Try throwing a die 6 times – you won't always get 1×6.) – when a cryptic note falls out of my text book:

You not on Facebook?

Not signed so don't know who wants to know. I could happily explain why I   choose not to to post photos of myself with my mouth puckered into a cat's arse and list the actresses I think I look like, or the boys I would like to shag. Or pretend that my age is sixteen and that I have a long list of friends, or that my relationship status is down for anything, up for anyone, or take stupid quizzes to identify my cartoon soulmate. Facebook is a marketing tool for posers. I am not a poser.

Facebook is still a huge deal in Belfast whereas in London everyone is into Instagram. I sometimes log on to take a peek at some of the girls from my old school to see what they are up to. They all seem to have silly poems about friendship and life, trying to sound deep and meaningful, like this one:

I MET U AS A STRANGER.
I TOOK U AS A FRiENd.
I HOPE WE MEET IN HEAVEN WHERE FRiENdSHiP NEVER ENDS.
SEND iT 2 of YR FRiENDS.

iF U GET 5 BAK UR A OK FRiENd
iF U GET 10 BAK UR A GREAT FRiENd
iF U GET 15 BAK UR A AWSOME FRiENd
iF U GET 20 UR dA BEST iN dA WHOLE WORLD

Not surprisingly no one ever mentions me, never mind contacts me, but that's how it goes – out of sight, out of mind. But then to be truthful I never really figured too highly on their agendas when I was there. Story of my life, it seems.

Matt has started to thaw. He has replied to my seventeenth text to say that he will consider resuming our friendship if I try to get Jessica Bailey's mobile number. He is seriously smitten.

Went to Nora's after school to walk the dogs. My shoulder is still aching from the experience. I think I have torn ligaments or popped my shoulder joint. I could barely keep hold of them as they strained on the leashes, so eager were they to make a run for it. I think they are programmed to think freedom is to be aspired to. It really was more a case of them walking me than the other way around.

The shelter has proved to be less than inspiring. The animals are obviously happy and well cared for, but the owner, Nora, is ill-tempered and unsociable. Not that she's said anything to upset me; it's just that she has a grouchy demeanour and never makes any effort to talk. She is kind of like the janitor in every episode of *Scooby Doo* – you know, solemn and mysterious and in a permanent bad mood.

I must confess I had expected the sort of shenanigans that go on in James Herriot books – not the sticking my arm up a cow's arse but more the sort of rescuing a canary from up the inside of a chimney, or finding a half-dead kitten in a ditch and giving it CPR. Instead I have to contend with the grouchy Nora.

Nora told me to be firm and shout 'heel' when the dogs try to pull away chasing doggy smells that make them overexcited, but it seems to have little effect. The truly hard part has been trying to keep them all together when I have to stop to clean up after they've done a poo. Gross! It's the law that you must pick up your dog's poo so being a good citizen I complied. Besides, I don't want to lose all my wages paying a doggy-doo fine.

Of course, when one dog stops to wee or do his doggy business the others think they can keep on walking, which proves to be rather difficult when I am trying to scoop up doggy poo while still being dragged along by a pack of dogs.

There I was, struggling to lift the offending matter and place it in the bright orange Sainsbury's carrier bag, a job which was tricky enough to do while trying to keep hold of four dogs and avoid dropping the poo all over my jeans, when I heard someone whistle in my direction. The fact that I was being watched while I did the scooping up job made it doubly hard. I looked up to see that the whistle had come from Ollie, one of Matt's mates. He raised his hand to say 'hi' in a gesture of recognition. I felt my cheeks flush with embarrassment for fear he was waving at someone other than me, but a quick sideways glance confirmed that he did indeed mean me.

The hot flush intensified when I realised I now had to stoop over and scrape dog poo off the pavement into the bag. Within seconds he had bounded up to me.

'All right,' he said, right up close, standing next to me.

'Oh, hi,' I managed, trying to control the dogs who were keen to jump all over Ollie to demonstrate doggy affection and welcome.

'Didn't know you had so many dogs,' he said smiling as he gave Toby, the scrawny greyhound, a scratch and a tussle behind his ear. Toby had been too old to race and had been left tied to a tree in the Botanic Gardens before someone found him and contacted Nora.

'Oh no, they're not mine. They're from the St Francis animal shelter. I'm working there part-time.' I was all pleased with myself for being able to say I was actually a person who works. Like I was a woman of means who didn't need a mother or a man to keep me. An independent, feminist warrior with a Sainsbury's bag filled with fresh, warm dog poo.

'Cool, beats working in Tesco's. You headed down the road?'

'Yeah, we're on our way back to the shelter.'

'Here, let me take a couple of these bad boys.' He expertly took hold of Molly's and Tess's leads. Instantly they seemed calmer. I think Ollie is maybe the Dog Whisperer's long-lost son. Have you ever seen that American guy (well, I think he's Hispanic but the show is filmed in America) on TV? He goes into homes with psychotic dogs, usually terriers who like attacking random things like shrubs and eating small children. He goes 'psst' at them a few times and they suddenly go all quiet and well behaved. Really he is teaching the owners how to be good dog disciplinarians since it's the dog owners who are at fault. The Whisperer helps them to see that by insisting Poochie wears a pink polka-dot bow and gets pushed about in a baby's pram, they are doing more damage than good to the doggie psyche. The dog learns to be a dog again and the owner learns to let it. And get this – the Dog Whisperer's name is Caesar! LOL.

Anyway, back to Ollie.

'Thanks,' I said, not knowing why I was blushing so furiously. I'm sure it was the raspberry red kind of embarrassment flushing. The kind that only people with red hair can achieve. He was just being friendly after all.

We headed down Botanic Avenue walking past the hordes of students from the nearby Queen's University.

I racked my mushy brain looking for something to say and stole a glance at Ollie but he seemed perfectly relaxed and at ease with himself, just happy to be walking along. His straw-blond hair seemed to catch the weak sunlight and his strong forearms, which had a light covering of blond hairs, controlled the dogs.

Walking along I tried to think of all the things I knew about Ollie:

He is one of Matt's mates;

He lives off the Lisburn Road – the posh side;

He is one of the few rugby players at school. This was one of the many anomalies I have found since moving to Belfast: as much as religion divides society, so too does your choice of sport. While both religions play soccer football, only Catholics play Gaelic football and nearly only Protestants play rugby. Matt had once referred to Ollie as a 'hun' since he plays rugby. All said in jest and humour, but like all banter of a political nature, I was convinced the remark had stung Ollie more than a little, but I don't really know why.

Sometimes I question Matt on the politics of Northern Ireland, trying to get a feel for the complexities of a nation which has seen long periods of civil unrest, but Matt is always flippant and makes some one-sided sectarian remark which only leaves me all the more confused.

We were approaching Nora's house when Ollie spoke. 'Will you be going to the party at Freya's house next weekend?'

I said, 'Not likely. I don't really get invited to those sorts of parties. Not that I mind. I'll probably be busy anyway.' I tried to sound nonchalant, but it might have come out all obnoxious like I wouldn't want to go even if I had been invited, which of course is total twat as I would love to go.

'Too bad. You could have come with me – I mean there's a crowd of us going and I'm sure Freya wouldn't mind if you tagged along.'

'Thanks, but like I said, I'll probably be busy. Right, here we are. Thanks for walking with me,' I said as we approached the driveway of Nora's dilapidated house. For some reason, I felt a bit embarrassed by the rundown exterior.

Ollie stroked the dogs' heads and then said, 'See you at school.'

'Yeah, bye.'

I took the leads from Ollie's hand and felt singed by his passing touch. God, what was wrong with me? I was acting so out of character. It was only Ollie. A boy I am used to seeing every day at school where he looks like every other boy – kind of dorky and up himself if truth be told.

**

Lonely Girl Blog

I'm putting myself up for adoption. Ate dinner with Kveta while watching a news report on fathers and the amount of time they spend with their children. The average father spends around ten minutes per day of quality time with their offspring. Report into child behaviour says this isn't adequate and that the neglectful fathers are responsible for a generation of knife carrying delinquents who will probably grow up to become politicians or some other dubious profession. Personally, I think ten minutes is rather generous. Back in a sec.

Right, just worked out that VM, my Virtual Mother, spends on average two minutes per day with me. I will grow up to be a reprobate or a solicitor.

Back again, just checking on Google to see if there is some sort of law which says this kind of neglectful parenting isn't allowed. Thought that at least there would be a European Commission for the rights of the child or the United Nations would have had some ruling to say you cannot spend less than ten minutes a day with your child, but sadly no. No such law exists, as obviously no one felt they had to legislate for such a circumstance. I am a legal loophole. Holly Willoughby, can you please adopt me?

Chapter 9

Croatian goulash and foxes

Wednesday 10.04am

Food sipped: one glass of tepid water

Lonely Girl Blog

I am in bed. V sick thanks I think to Kveta's cooking. She cooked a sort of goulash dish on Tuesday night and we ate it in companionable silence while watching the news. She *tsked* at every report and said something in Croatian when a report about Brexit and the border came on.

Last night I woke with intense stomach pains, so bad it felt like someone was twisting my insides. I actually crawled to my mother's room in desperation. Of course, she was in Dublin. Kveta eventually heard my moans and helped me back to bed where I threw up.

Croatian goulash does not look nice the second time round. It was 4am before we had my bed changed and me cleaned up. The pains came and went. Kveta must be made of sterner stuff than me for she hasn't felt as much as a twinge. I am sure it was the goulash though coz I know she tries to always buy the reduced-price items. I've seen the evidence – packets of meat that are best before the day she buys them, along with battered packets of vegetables that don't look fit for consumption. She must pocket the money left over from the housekeeping my mother gives her. I should be more alert, she could be feeding me roadkill for all I know. Come to think of it, the goulash could have been made from the grey squirrels I see darting around the garden.

In the morning Kveta phoned Stella, who set about organising the coven to pop in and check on me. The doctor was called and pills were dispensed to help the stomach ache. Joni fussed about while chatting to someone on her mobile, telling them how poor little Tara was seriously ill and Stella couldn't possibly come home since she had an editorial meeting.

I slept on and off and remember talking to Stella on the phone at one point. She told me if I felt worse I was to call Nora. What she thought Nora could do for me I don't know. I could imagine her praying over her statue of St Francis and sprinkling me with holy water and possibly giving me a worming tablet.

I dreamt of Nora and her animals all running riot in our house. The parrot was eating one of Stella's hats and the canaries kept flying into Kveta's silky black hair and getting all tangled. I couldn't get out of bed to calm them down but I didn't seem to care. Feel a bit spacey but better than I was.

Lonely Girl Blog

Nora said I can feed the fox next time and she let me name her – Roxy. Have been reading up on foxes.

Things I have found out about foxes:

In the wild, red foxes seldom live for more than seven years, but in captivity they live for up to fifteen years.

Red foxes are widespread across Europe (but absent from Iceland), Canada, the USA, and in Asia from Japan to China. They were introduced to Australia.

Red foxes are opportunistic feeders i.e. they eat what they can find. They also eat insects, earthworms, fruit, berries, wild birds, small mammals and scraps left by humans. Nora said she feeds Roxy scraps and sometimes dog food.

They are not endangered and are the most widespread wild carnivore in the world.

Red foxes are primarily active at dusk and at night. They are solitary but they very occasionally group together in a pack.

Vixens come into heat once a year for one to six days. They give birth to four to seven cubs in a den (also called an earth) after a gestation period (pregnancy) of 51-53 days. The cubs are weaned after seven to nine weeks and become sexually mature after a year.

Comments from blog readers:

Note to Jacques Meov: I have forwarded your offer of adoption to Interpol. I am sure they will be in touch. Please do not leave me a message again.

Madonna: thank you very much for your kind offer but unfortunately, I don't think I could convert to Kabalah as I am not mad on those red string bracelet thingies.

Victoria: also thank you for contacting me but don't think I could in all conscience accept your offer as it wouldn't work out – I would never be able to look at Brooklyn as a brother – it would be soooo wrong.

Stella

My baby was poorly. Really sick. That Wildling au pair gave her food poisoning and my poor baby had to suffer the most awful tummy cramps. I would sack her if I didn't need her so badly. It takes three months to find a new au pair and with Brexit the pickings are slim. I guess the Wildling will have to stay.

I must not feel guilty. It is my duty to work, to be a fulfilled career woman. I am setting Tara a good example. She will grow up to know that she doesn't have to depend on a man to keep her in Wolf and Badger clothing. As Beyoncé would say: 'If you are not feeling your best self, you must address the issues and treat yourself well.'

Well, Queen B, I hear you, and I treated myself to some new clothes and a few accessories.

Note to self: check if Wolf and Badger stuff I ordered last week has arrived in Belfast. I do love a late-night order arriving to cheer me up.

The situation with Nora has worked out well. Tara loves working with the smelly animals and it makes me feel less under pressure to be organising outings. I can't be facilitating Tara's every activity.

Chapter 10

Bad smells and scary religious pictures

Tara

*Food consumed: scrambled eggs, toast dripping with butter much to
Stella's annoyance, latte, Mikado biscuits – one packet, salad with
grilled chicken breast and balsamic dressing.*

Lonely Girl Blog

Nora was occupied with clipping Maisie's toenails when I
arrived at the shelter. The dog yelped as if being tortured
but I knew from experience that Maisie was just protesting,
she didn't really mind her nails being cut. Nora had her bundled
under one arm while she endeavoured to trim the nails with the
other. I stepped forward and helped to hold Maisie steady.

'Good girl, there you go,' said Nora, leaving me in no doubt
that Maisie was the one receiving the praise, not me.

I have been coming to the shelter for a couple of months now
and I can't really say I have learnt much about Nora beyond the
fact that she is obsessive about her animals and that she is fervently
religious.

Most of my time is spent walking the dogs and cleaning out
hutches. The inside of the house creeps me out. Statues of Virgin
Marys and the infant Jesus lurk in unexpected places – corners
and above cupboards – looking down with their all-knowing eyes.
Even the bathroom has a sort of shrine to Saint Bernadette. I
must confess to feeling most uncomfortable trying to pee with

Bernadette staring intently at me, an expression of pure adoration on her chiselled face and her arms stretched out, reaching to me in welcome.

The Sacred Heart picture hanging on the landing wall is the scariest of all. It is an image of the Jesus figure displaying his bloodied hands, punctured by the nails from the crucifixion. A thick band of horny thorns is embedded in his head. If that isn't frightening enough, worse still, the picture shows his heart crushed by thorns and bleeding. It is truly gruesome. When I told Matt about it he merely shrugged and said his gran had the same picture in her living room, which reminded me yet again of another peculiarity of living in Belfast. In the two years I have lived here I have seen more religious icons and union flags than I have ever seen during my entire time living in London or Leeds.

It is clear that Nora lives in chaos. She has a routine for her animals but no sense of order in her home. She seems to eat when hungry; breakfast can be at noon and dinner can be at eight at night. From the leftover dinner plates I see stacked in the sink she seems to exist on hastily made sandwiches and cheese. Empty milk cartons, egg boxes and any old bits and bobs lie strewn around the kitchen. Unopened post is stacked on the counter in a haphazard pile, until it is so big that a landslide sends it flying to the floor where the dogs promptly walk all over it all leaving muddy paw prints. But apart from the darkness, the religious icons and the mess, it is the smell which is most perturbing. I have tried to identify the odour and have, through a process of sniff and eliminate, come to believe it is coming from the floorboards. I am beginning to wonder if some creature has crawled under there and been forgotten. It is very possible; there are so many animals I don't know how Nora keeps account of them all.

I decided to sort out the kitchen. I have pledged to myself and the Sacred Heart picture that every weekend I will give myself an extra job – clean the cooker, clear away any empty bottles, change the bin, stack the old newspapers in an orderly pile for recycling, find the bad smell – that sort of thing.

After I made some sort of impression on the kitchen I moved on to the living room. Close inspection showed signs of damp in the corners of the ceiling. The fusty, dead smell couldn't be eradicated by fresh air alone. But still I swept up and dusted and rearranged the furniture so that the room seemed brighter and bigger without too much effort. If only I could rely on Nora to keep it that way. The trouble is that Nora seems to be genuinely uninterested in anything beyond her animals and going to Mass. Life outside her home seems to confuse her and she positively bristles when anyone dares to ring the doorbell.

How mum managed to secure the job for me, I don't know. I must remember to ask Stella how she met Nora. I can't imagine how they could have known each other. Someone connected to the magazine must have heard about the job and told Stella. It's a bit strange. Still, I am glad it has come my way. Despite Nora's gruff mannerisms and air of arrogance, I do like her. She is selfless in her devotion to the animals and her hard exterior melts away the minute she's talking to one of her dogs or cats. Suddenly the frown lines relax and the wrinkles around her mouth and eyes become softened into creases as her whole face lights up into a warm smile.

She rarely praises my work but seems grateful for an extra pair of hands. She always pays me on time, without hesitation, and checks that I will be back the following week. I am sure that Nora needs me. Walking the dogs is obviously too strenuous a task for her and regular phone calls asking for a place for a stray seem to make her nerves jangle. I am a welcome, if un-thanked addition.

Thursday 5.55pm

Food gorged: two pop tarts, one apple, one banana milkshake, one slice of school canteen pizza, Kveta's stew stuff, one Star Bar and one glass of milk.

Lonely Girl Blog

Arrived home from school to find a brown fabric bag lying on my perfectly made-up bed. Eyed it with suspicion. Stella likes to leave unexpected packages to ease her guilt at being a long-distance mother, but usually the gifts are far removed from my hemisphere of taste and they just prove to be more useless trinkets or clothes to hang like limp scarecrows in my already bulging wardrobe.

This time Stella has trumped herself in hideousness. The bag contained a pair of Self Portrait oversized, overpriced white patent troll-like footwear. My heart sank. Would Stella never accept that I didn't want gifts, especially not the type which cost more than it would take to feed Nora's animals for a week?

Nike Air is the chosen footwear of the Jessica Bailey crowd. I've seen them slouching along the Lisburn Road, wearing their petrol-coloured trainers teamed with their Abercrombie and Fitch hoodies and tight jeans like a uniform. Their hair is invariably straightened poker straight or tousled with great care into a bed-head mess and topped with a beanie hat or a crocheted sequined beret. Any sign of individuality seems to be eliminated. Not that it bothers Matt. He is still smitten and Jessica's pillowy lips and snub pug nose are all he can think about. Of course, I am sure he has thought about Jessica's rounded high breasts and her denim clad ass just as much.

The sad thing is I used to have Matt marked down as a smart guy. He always does well in tests without the need to swot up, yet at the first swing of Jessica's long lemon-blonde hair he becomes a gibbering moron, blinded to reason by his sex hormones.

Still, who am I to dismiss his infatuation? It's clear to me that boys prefer the Jessica Baileys of the world to the plain Taras. I've grown up with ginger hair and the inference has always been that red hair is something to be pitied and ashamed of, or at least a little resentful of. Over the years it has darkened down to a rich chestnut-auburn colour – sort of the colour of conkers – but I will always be a ginger head. Boys like blondes or girls with intense dark brown hair. They like girls like Jessica or Freya who carry their pert breasts with pride and sashay down the corridor at school as if it is a catwalk. I don't like attracting attention to myself and I wouldn't even know how to begin to flirt.

I have listened to the easy banter between Matt, Ollie and Luke with Jessica's crowd and can't fathom the jokey name calling and the insults. The inane girly giggles and the boys' faked nonchalance leaves me cold. And a bit resentful, like I am the only one not to get the joke.

I slung the boots onto the floor and lay back on my bed. I love my room, my own private sanctuary.

One thing Stella has always been good at is creating a nice room for me. When I was four or five, as a surprise, Stella arranged for one of her friends who worked as a set designer to paint fairies and elves all over the walls. It was like sleeping in an enchanted forest. Then when we moved to London, she paid a decorator to create a wizards and witches theme which delighted me as I was enthralled with the Harry Potter books at the time. Life with Stella has never been boring, but at times I have wished for something a little closer to normality.

'Well, did they fit?' asked Stella later that night.

'Sure, yeah, thanks, but Mum, I didn't need new boots.'

'Honey, they're not just boots, they're Self Portrait ankle boots with an angled heel and a wrap-round formation. Besides, a girl can never have too many pairs of shoes or boots. Now come here and tell me what you've been up to this week?'

I padded across the cherry wood floor in what Stella calls the family room and sat down on the oversized brown leather couch beside my mother. I drew my legs up under myself and wrapped my arms around my knees.

'Not a lot, just the usual – school, hanging out with Kveta, went to Starbucks with Matt and dropped into the shelter to help Nora out for an extra couple of hours.'

'So how are you getting on with Nora?' she asked.

'Grand, I just do as she asks. She keeps herself to herself, but I love working there with all the animals. We had a parrot delivered last week. It had been so badly cared for it was practically bald from plucking its own feathers,' I said, thinking how pitiful the poor bird had looked and how careful and gentle Nora had been in coaxing it out of its cage. She had made soft low cooing noises to reassure the poor bird.

'Do you find her a bit strange? Over the top, like, with all the religious stuff?' asked Stella.

'At first, but I've got used to her and now I see she's just lonely and not used to having people around her. There's no harm in her really. She's a bit like Rosie, the dog, her bark's worse than her bite.'

'Good, glad it's worked out,' Stella said, picking up her iPad with a finality which suggested I could leave. Mummy time was over.

'You never said how you came to find out about the job,' I said, suddenly unsure if I should probe without even knowing why.

And she replied all casual like. 'Oh, Nora is just someone I knew from when I grew up in Belfast. I knew her a long time ago.'

Lonely Girl Blog
11.55pm

Can't sleep. Kveta's TV is so loud it's keeping me awake. I don't like to complain coz I feel sorry for her as she truly has no life beyond *Game of Thrones*.

When I can't sleep I work on my graphic novel. I rest my sketchbook against the wall and stand back to get a better perspective of my work. It is difficult to capture the sense of claustrophobia and yet cosiness I want the cave to convey. The story arc follows the longing of the teenage girl Shyla's need to explore the world beyond the underground cave where she lives, sheltered from the harsh rays of the sun. While the cave is her home and the only world she knows, Shyla longs to break free and find her own place in a world left ruined by ecological disaster. Hang on, I want to add a bit to the cave – I don't think the fire will work if they don't have some sort of chimney.

12.16am

I'm back. Stella's comments about Nora have left me feeling uneasy. I've tried to lose myself in my drawing instead of dwelling on the conversation with Stella about Nora. I didn't know why but I am suspicious and perturbed by Stella having known Nora years ago. I just would never have put the two of them together in a million years. The ultra-organised, groomed to perfection Stella is so far removed from the crazed, edgy Nora.

They could never have been friends. Perhaps they had been neighbours at one time. That must be it. Still, I have the strangest sense that there's more to it and for some reason it worries me.

Stella

I'm delighted that Tara's little part-time job is working out. Hopefully it will help her appreciate the luxury of writing for a living instead of doing actual work. I can't see why she would enjoy cleaning up after animals but it appears that she does. It's probably just a phase she is going through.

Right, back to work. I have to write a feature on Millie Bobby Brown and her ten best outfits. For once my fashion mojo is waning. It's difficult to conjure up six hundred odd interesting words on the fashion choices of a teenage actress when I'm feeling a little jaded.

Reasons why I'm feeling low:

- I don't have a man in my life.
- It can be lonely going home alone at the end of a party.
- There is no one to take the bin out on a Thursday night.

- I need to find other ways to feel fulfilled. Still haven't committed to the tattoo yet. It should be meaningful and reflect a significant time in my life. I need to do more research. I know! I shall write a feature on celebrity tattoos and kill two birds with one stone.

Tara
Saturday 6.35pm

Food devoured: carrot sticks, grapes, oatcakes, rice cakes, latte, blueberry muffin x one.

Lonely Girl Blog

Matt has come out of hiding. It must be said, despite having been at risk of third-degree facial burns and permanent scarring, his skin has never looked better. Once the chemical peel had worn off and his fresh, new epidermis (we are looking at the skin as an organ in Biology) was exposed, he was delighted with his positively glowing complexion.

He took me to Starbucks to say thanks and sorry for being such a jerk. It wasn't my fault after all. I had only done what he asked. Still, I won't be going near any of that facial stuff again.

While we were supping our hot drinks and eating blueberry muffins, who should arrive but the Jessica Bailey crowd. There were four others with Jess – Freya, Andrea, Ella, and Lisa, all looking like made-up extras from that old show *Gossip Girl* – all ultra-styled and slick. Of course, Matt nearly choked on his hot chocolate and immediately began talking in a loud voice to attract attention. This was really embarrassing since his voice is breaking and every third word came out like a high-pitch choirboy.

Why does he allow Jess to have such an effect on him? Can't he just be cool about it? I can understand he fancies her. God, if I was a fella, I'd probably fancy her too, but I would hope to have enough dignity not to make it as pathetically obvious. Naturally

Jess and her friends acted like we didn't exist, which only made Matt speak louder and higher. I felt like crawling under the table in embarrassment for him.

Monday 5.05pm

Food nibbled: breadsticks with cheese spread, three olives, one sweet potato with Kveta's slop.

Lonely Girl Blog

We had a careers class today. Mr McWacken (I kid you not – Wacky McWacken is his nickname) asked us to fill in a questionnaire to discover what our ideal career is.

According to Mr McWacken's wisdom I should consider a career in dentistry, banking, financial accounting (is there any other type?) or biomedical research. Since I hate maths and don't exactly do well in science I fail to see how he came up with this estimation. When I told him I wanted to be a graphic novelist, he looked confused and said that I could be a graphic designer and write a novel in my spare time. LOL.

Note to Space Hopper who left a question on this blog referring to my origins. Like my mother, I was born in Belfast, I travelled around Central America until I was one, moved to Leeds when I was a baby where I lived until I was seven, before moving to London until we transferred to Belfast nearly two years ago. Stella's career dictates where we live but with her current job at *Heart* magazine I insisted we stayed in Belfast, so she commutes to Dublin.

I am old enough to have a say in where I live and although I don't necessarily prefer Belfast over Leeds or London, at least I have a chance of getting to know the city and perhaps making some friends beyond Matt. Hope that answers your query, Space Hopper, and don't try tracking me down in a weirdo paedo way. We have been warned in PSD (Personal and Social Development) at school about giving away too much geographical and personal information while online, so bugger off!

Major differences between London and Belfast:

1. No one notices you in London, even if you walk down the street wearing fluorescent green tights and a pink wig and you're a man.
2. Everyone notices everything in Belfast and everyone seems to know everyone else or at least their cousin.
3. Belfast has few black or Indian people but plenty of eastern Europeans and Chinese.
4. Belfast has no transvestites that I am aware of whereas I have seen five at different times in London. Asked Stella about this once and she said that was coz Belfast trannies play dress up in the privacy of their own home for fear of ridicule from twisted old grannies who would disapprove or DUP councillors.
5. London has lots of homeless people whereas Belfast doesn't seem to have too many. I have seen the odd one sitting selling *The Big Issue* in town.
6. London can have really hot days and Belfast can have really wet days.
7. It is so much easier to eat out cheaply in London.
8. Belfast doesn't have congestion charges, Big Ben or the Queen.
9. Instead Belfast has Stormont, the Albert Clock, and bonfires.
10. History in Belfast can mean last week.
11. Even colours in Belfast have political connotations: green is nationalist, orange is unionist. Note to Secretary of State – this is useful information.

Chapter 11

Peeing and being back stabbed by the Bitches of Belfast

Tara
Tuesday 4.35pm

Lonely Girl Blog

My life just got worse.

This is what happened:

It was lunch break and I had gone to the loos to wee. No biggie, you might say. So what? Well, there I was, sat with my knickers round my ankles, when I heard them. The Bitches of Belfast. I willed myself not to pee for fear of alerting the voices on the other side of the toilet door of my presence.

'She really thinks she's something – just coz her mother works for a magazine doesn't mean she can dress well or look good.'

'God, did you see the lame braids she came into school with today? What age does she think she is? Seven?' Then laughter, bitchy, snide giggles.

Stupidly I put my hand up to my plaits in defence. I thought they looked cool this morning.

'She is a complete melter. The ginger minger. If she had any sense she would have highlighted her hair by now and has she never heard of face powder to cover those freckles?'

'Don't get me started on her English accent.'

'And the way she keeps hanging around Matt. He can never get rid of her – she's always mooning after him like a love-sick puppy.'

'Speaking of dogs, did you hear she is hanging out at that animal shelter on Astoria Road? God, the smell of that place when you walk by, it's revolting.'

'Have you seen the old hag who lives there? She is like some sort of witch, thinks she can cure sick animals with witchcraft.'

'Maybe they're related.'

Hoots of laughter echoed around the tiled walls, bouncing back at me.

There it was: the raspberry red heat of shame but this time mingled with pure anger rising up my body. How dare they? Nora did harm to no one. She didn't deserve their disrespect and come to think of it, neither did I. What have I ever done to any of them?

Hot tears threatened to spill down my face. I bit my bottom lip to maintain some sort of composure. I didn't want to have to go into French class with a blotchy face and swollen eyelids. The bell rang out, announcing that break time was over. I waited until I was sure they had left and finally peed. Flushed the loo and went to wash my hands. I could scarcely bring myself to look at my reflection in the mirror for fear of unleashing the overwhelming sadness I felt. I knew they were cruel, mean and vacuous, but it didn't make their comments any less hurtful.

I was glad to have Nora's house to go to after school. I didn't feel like eating Kveta's cooking and I didn't want to see Matt. Maybe he had been the one to complain about me hanging around him. He could have said something to Ollie or Luke and they could have mentioned it to one of the Jessica crowd, now forever known as the Bitches of Belfast.

Either way I am not going to be seen 'mooning' around after him. I have better things to do with my time.

Rosie, the beagle, has had a litter of pups and Nora has been trying without much luck to rehome them. I have had a really good idea though – to set up a website for the shelter. We could advertise pets looking for homes and raise much-needed funds to keep the shelter going. I could design the website myself and maintain it.

I would love it but I know that Nora has a natural reluctance to anything outside her realm of church and animals.

I also wanted to ask Nora about Stella, to try to decipher how they had come to know each other. When I questioned Stella over the weekend I was met with a stony 'don't go there' reply. It doesn't make much sense.

As usual Stella has been preoccupied with work for the magazine. Even more than usual. The new season has brought with it many fashion conundrums Stella has to solve – like how to keep your feet cool in Uggs and how to wear the new yellows without looking like a canary – so I let it go. Still I am curious, and I wanted to see what Nora had to say about my mother.

So I casually dropped Stella into the conversation with Nora. Mentioned that Stella had said she had known Nora from long ago and I swear Nora literally froze like her statue of Mary at the bottom of the garden. It was as if I had blasphemed in front of one of her holy pictures.

She turned and said, 'That's one way of putting it,' before shuffling off upstairs.

Later I asked her if I could help with the administration side of the shelter. 'If you're looking more money, I don't have it,' she said, her eyes narrowing to slits of suspicion.

I assured her I was only trying to be helpful. Still, I think she mellowed when she saw me trawling through the neglected paperwork she handed to me. I separated the bills from the junk mail and tried to put them in some sort of order – starting with those that seemed to be more pressing than others. I think the electric bill needs to be paid first though I doubt Nora would notice if they cut her off. She seems to rise at dawn and go to bed early. She keeps warm wearing layers of moth-eaten jumpers and with scarves wrapped around her neck.

Then on the way home from Nora's the creepiest thing happened. I found an envelope sellotaped to the bus stop with my name printed on it in large felt-tip blue capitals. I couldn't avoid it and even though my name was on it I still looked about me before peeling it off and opening it.

Inside on a sheet of file a paper it said: 'Are you on Snapchat? Can't find an email address for you, don't want to ask about. Set up an account and we could chat.'

Feeling really weirded out now. Who could have known I would be walking past that particular bus stop?

If there are any sickos reading my blog and are leaving me notes to find – back off. I will report you to the PSNI or ChildLine. You have been warned.

Pop Tart has just left a message asking if I told Matt how mean the Jessica crowd were in the toilets. The answer, Pop Tart, is no, what would be the point? He would only agree with them and tell me that my image is all wrong and I need to lighten up. I don't want to give him the satisfaction of knowing they were talking about him anyway, even if it was only to say what a saddo hanger-on I am to him.

Chapter 12

Who do you think you are?

Stella

Tara tossed that glorious hair of hers and flounced out of the kitchen. I merely suggested that she registers for an extras acting agency and she lost it. I had to endure a ten-minute lecture on how I have no clue as to what my daughter is interested in. Then she declares that I deliberately push her into arenas where she is going to fail.

'Why would you fail?'

'Because I don't look like an actress. I am not pretty enough,' she said.

She truly has no notion at all of how beautiful she is. How is it possible that I have brought her up with no self-worth? It is my biggest failing as a mother to have not instilled in my child that she is the most beautiful girl in the world. I know brains are important, personality matters, and kindness trumps the lot, but everyone knows we just say those things. Tara is one of those special people who have no idea how they impact on the world. It is my responsibility to lay out opportunities in her path. I must speak to Sammy about orchestrating a little perk of the job treat for her. She needs to see what others see when they look at her.

Must make sure I do interesting things with my week. My number of Instagram followers hasn't risen for a week and I need to find a brand aesthetic that will work for me. Twinkling fairy lights draped over everything is so last season. I need to find some natural foliage. I could arrange lots of branches and maybe I could hang little jam jars with lit candles in them. It would make a pretty back drop for pics of me. Maybe Tara would like a trip to the Botanic Gardens to pilfer some trees?

My week: Work, commute from Belfast, three events to attend in Dublin, a theatre outing, and a Friday night fake away and catch up with Tara. Fake away consisted of rice noodles and stir fry tofu.

Must remember to do that hot yoga class on Sunday morning.

It's Friday night and I'm at the Perch Bar in Belfast. It's a rooftop bar kitted out with comfy sofas, blankets to keep warm and lots of bird paraphernalia. The girls are getting the drinks in. I'm tasked with getting some seats, which means elbowing my way through the twenty-somethings. I'm preoccupied. Tara has been spending too much time at Nora's. Initially I thought it would be good for her. They could get to know each other on their own terms. Now I'm worried that it's all going to backfire on me spectacularly. Nothing else for it but to down a few vodka tonics. A bit of music and the warmth of the alcohol will dispel my worries. It usually does the trick.

Tara

Food: Porridge, dried mango slices, sausage roll, can of Coke, cheese and ham sandwich with pickle stuff, Kveta's homemade fish fingers – don't ask.

I have tried Stella's phone three times. It's switched off. Damn. I need to speak to her. She won't be home until Thursday.

Usually our arrangement suits me just fine. I never actually *need* Stella. Kveta takes care of the washing and ironing. I can always make myself something to eat if Kveta's cooking proves to be too scary. I also like the freedom to potter about the house without feeling I have to make conversation and give answers to the usual predictable questions of how was your day and what did you learn at school?

Matt is always envious of my set-up. He doesn't appreciate the joys of having a conventional mother. Instead he complains that

I'm a waster, who never uses my domestic set up to my advantage and organise parties and wild sleepovers. Problem is I have no one to invite beyond Matt.

But for once I wish that Stella was home. It isn't often that I actually want to talk to her. The thing is I need to ask her about Nora. It isn't really something that could be discussed over the phone, or on Skype, but in the absence of having a face to face discussion I may have no choice. Hang on, I'll try her phone again.

No good, it's going straight to voicemail.

Here's the thing:

I had been happily sorting through Nora's usual assortment of junk mail and money off vouchers which had been stuffed into an obviously long-neglected kitchen drawer, when I came across a pile of unopened post. The letter on the top caught my eye, for there on the front I saw in bold type 'Mrs Margaret Hunter'. Hunter is my surname. (Paedos, stalkers and weirdos look away now. I do not want you using my name to track me down, kidnap me and hold me a prisoner in some daggy garden shed and do unthinkable things to my feet or any other part of my anatomy.)

I just stood there holding the envelope. Hunter. The same name. Then the penny dropped – we could be related.

Looking for answers I started to trawl through the drawer until I found a brown manila envelope full of old photographs.

Yes, okay, I know I shouldn't be nosy, but what is the harm in having a peek? There were plenty of photos of cats and a few dogs, even a parakeet sitting on a bald man's head. A few were obviously taken in the garden long before it had become so overgrown and unkempt. But it was the fifth photo in the pile made me start suddenly, as if I had seen a ghost. I felt an icy finger of nervousness snake down my spine, for there, staring out at me from the old, perfectly square coloured photograph was none other than my own mother.

There was Stella, as a young girl, smiling widely at the camera with her arm wrapped around what must surely be a younger more presentable and groomed Nora.

They seemed so at ease and comfortable with each other, like they were the best of friends. The picture was obviously fairly old. Stella looked not much older than I am now. She was wearing a purple turtleneck jumper and wide flared jeans. A silver necklace was hanging from her neck. Her hair was long and curly and her feet were bare, standing on a green swirly-patterned carpet, probably the same one in the living room now except sunlight has faded it to a dull mossy green and the cats and dogs have worn patches of it threadbare.

Behind Nora, I could see a tinsel-covered Christmas tree with its Quality Street coloured fairy lights twinkling merrily. Someone had written something on the back of the picture for the writing had pushed through making an indention across the image.

I turned it round and looked at the back: 'Christmas Day 1985'.

Everything seemed to shift around me. It was like being on that programme 'Who Do You Think You Are' and unearthing old family documents to find that the family I thought I knew, was really something quite different all together.

I sort of felt like Alice in Wonderland, falling through the rabbit hole only to find herself in another world were everything was altered. It was as if I was looking through a kaleidoscope and had adjusted the lens making the image suddenly fall into sharp focus showing me a new picture, an image I had never seen before and one that seemed so peculiar it made no sense at all.

Virtual mother has a man friend
Tara

Food swallowed: Rice Krispies x 2 bowls, two flapjack peanut butter sandwiches, one can of club orange, one tin of tuna fish, 2 croissants with blueberry jam.

Lonely Girl Blog

As if my life isn't desperate enough. I am the social outcast of school. Matt has taken to hanging around the back of the canteen in the hope of looking cool enough for Jessica Bailey to notice him; I keep finding anonymous notes in strange places; I am living with a reclusive au pair who has taken to her room, rarely coming out unless directly asked to and worse, much worse than anything else, my mother has a boyfriend.

Can my life be any more desperate? You may ask. Yes, for the boyfriend in question is none other than Dylan McKay; for those of you not familiar with the Dublin social scene, Dylan McKay is the newest, hottest, happening, hip model-wannabe actor.

What he sees in my ageing mother is beyond me, but perhaps her occupation and her ability to drop his name into as many column inches as she likes could be part of the attraction.

As if it wasn't bad enough that Stella is only a part-time, virtual mother, I now have to share our weekend time with Dylan McKay. They expect me to have dinner with them in fancy restaurants like the Merchant Hotel and Coco's and then drop me home before they go for drinks in the Apartment and finish up clubbing in Sirens. What's worse, they think nothing of eating each other's faces in front of me – does she not understand that I am an impressionable teenager? And then there are the sounds that go bump in the night – *I do not want to go there!*

Can anyone out there advise me on how best to explain to my mother that I may actually need her to be more motherly and less like a rebellious big sister?

Your thoughts would be gratefully appreciated. Except for Micer who is verging on the creepy – keep your comments to yourself, mate.

5.05pm

In response to blog reader Jiggy's query, Stella's preoccupation with the gorgeous Dylan McKay has prevented me from probing about Nora. How could I ask her personal questions about our unspoken family history while he was nibbling on my mother's ear, or lying sprawled out on our sofa flicking through the music channels?

Besides, Stella has become a simpering lapdog to him, waiting on him and seeing to his every whim. Urgh, just the thought of it is enough to make me gag.

Pathetic. Why do relationships have to render people brain dead and moronic? I see enough of it with Matt without witnessing the same pathetic lovelorn behaviour being carried out by my own mother, in my own home.

Since I have been forced to wait and bide my time with the questions, I have begun to have second thoughts on bringing the subject up at all. Maybe there's a reasonable explanation as to why Nora would have a photograph of Stella taken on Christmas Day – they didn't have to be related to be spending Christmas together. Do they? Maybe I wanted it to be true. Maybe my hidden desire to be part of a family has made me see something that wasn't actually there. I have somehow made it so. I've have tried it out in my mind – Nora is related to me. No, it doesn't fit. Nora with her wild gypsy hair, animal stench and hoarding is the antithesis of my slick, organised, on-trend mother.

No matter how I twist the images around in my mind I can't make them settle into anything other than absurdity. Perhaps there is a far-flung family tree connection? That is as far as I can contrive the image. My hand darts to my chest and I can feel my heart flutter like the wings of one of Nora's canaries. I feel like I've tripped and fallen into an alternate universe. Whatever the truth is, I have to find out.

Stella has always been vague about her background. I know she was born and brought up in Belfast. I suppose I have always been accepting of the fact that we didn't have an extended family to visit. Growing up in Leeds, I never questioned why we didn't visit Belfast. It was just an accepted fact that it was always just the two of us.

When the opportunity to move to Belfast arose Stella had been apprehensive. It was clear to me that she wanted to go but needed constant reassurance that I was okay with it. I had taken time to think about it. Perhaps I would suddenly find a long-lost family and be welcomed back into the bosom of family parties and cosy Christmas scenes. It would make a change from just being the two of us, especially on Christmas Day when there's never exactly been an abundance of pressies under the tree. But when I did raise the issue of meeting family back in Belfast, Stella told me not to go expecting too much and anyway, what was wrong with there being just the two of us? Sure, she had said, she had good friends from her schooldays in Belfast and they would be like family to us. Initially the job at *Heart* magazine was based in Belfast. We didn't bank on Stella's quick promotion to the fashion editor post and requirement to be in Dublin most of the week. But the new set-up suited us. Stella had her independence and I was content to let Kveta pick up after me and *tsk tsk* when she was annoyed.

I sort of feel now that it's best to keep my head down and pretend nothing has changed. Except now I will be on heightened alert to pick up any clues.

Stella

I've bagged myself a man. Hoorah! We met at an after party in some random warehouse off the Ormeau Road. It was a select gathering. All writers, film crew and A-listers only. Believe it or not, Belfast has a good ratio of hot famous people since the filming of *The Fall* and *Game of Thrones*. The infrastructure is in place for other big movie productions so we are actually teeming with good pickings. Not that I was looking. It was a work night event and I was on my best behaviour when I was introduced to up-and-coming actor Dylan McKay. It was one of those encounters when his pheromones slam into your pheromones and everything else is irrelevant. Things I remember from that night: he smelt delicious, like a ripe pear mingled with an animal muskiness. His chest was smooth and hairless, well-toned rather than brawny, and he had nicely defined arms. He kissed like an amateur, all tongue and gushy, but I just directed him down below and that worked out perfectly well.

When I woke the next day to find myself pleasantly tired and exhilarated I thought that was the end of it. Dylan was all for having breakfast and meeting up later on so for once I thought, feck it, why not?

Tara is older now and I can't stay single for ever. I have been the dutiful mother and denied myself my womanly needs for long enough. The odd date in Dublin doesn't count as Tara doesn't meet them. That morning in bed, Dylan looked like a new puppy, frisky and cute. How could I resist?

Chapter 13

Tara

Coven view Dylan and another anonymous note

Food gobbled: Two rounds of toast, one packet of hubba bubba, one chicken tikka salad roll, one bowl of pasta with tomato sauce, six chocolate strawberries.

Lonely Girl Blog

The coven has been summoned to view Dylan. Elise, Maura and Joni all trooped in clutching flowers (an exotic display of black and orange blooms which looked strangely sinister), a bottle of wine and a platter of strawberries dipped in dark chocolate – they are Joni's speciality.

I almost felt sorry for Dylan as they cooed and ahhed over him like he was a new handbag Stella had purchased from Brown Thomas.

As he walked across the kitchen to open the wine, Maura all but strained her neck in a bid to check out his bum, giving Stella the thumbs up in appreciation. Stella was grinning, clearly delighted to be dating the almost famous Dylan McKay, ten years her junior. She has taken to overseeing his career, promising to introduce him to all the movers and shakers north of the border with a hope of eventually exporting him to London. She needn't think she's going with him. I am not moving again. Besides, as soon as Dylan achieves any sort of stardom you can be sure Stella will be given her notice: services no longer required.

There was an awkward moment when Elise remarked how Dylan was closer in age to her seventeen-year-old daughter Rachel, than to Stella.

Elise: 'My God, but I should introduce you to her and you two could hit it off and have a blast together!'

Stella was not impressed. She gave Elise the mad evil eye (not to be taken lightly) and put a possessive hand on Dylan's knee.

Found another note: 'Are you still dog walking? Might bump into you.'

This time it had been slipped into my blazer pocket. Greatly relieved to think it had to be someone from school and that it can't be some cyber-stalker reading this blog, before I realised that perhaps one of my teachers is the pervert in question. Mr McGimpsey looks like he doesn't have a life beyond a computer screen. I could imagine him tapping away at a keyboard in a lonely bedsit. So, Mr McGimpsey, if it is you, back away from the computer screen NOW. I am not an impressionable teenager willing to be groomed.

Note to Pop Tart: I know my mother has a life of her own to live but surely it is not unreasonable to expect her to be a little less in my face with her latest toy boy conquest. I know she has avoided long-term relationships because of me and that I am now of an age when I am expected to be mature about these things, but could she not act a bit more her age? It upsets the natural equilibrium of life. For instance, school is a microcosm of society, right? Say I start going out with a first year, or worse, someone from primary school, there'd be uproar. It just isn't the done thing.

I am not expecting too much. Am I?

Debating whether or not to dye my hair. Should I lighten it at the suggestion of the Bitches from Belfast or should I take a stand for redheads everywhere and remain au naturel? Thoughts appreciated.

Chapter 14

Council officialdom and the bra nest threat

Saturday 4.58pm
Tara

*Food swallowed: two croissants, one banana, one chocolate milkshake,
one burger with tomato relish, one KitKat, one Wagon Wheel.*

Lonely Girl Blog

Woke early and let myself drift in and out of sleep.
Although I had to be at Nora's by ten, I was enjoying
the sweetness of having a lie in. Some of my best ideas
come when I am drifting in the ether between waking and sleep.
My imagination can explore the dry tundra of the cave dwellers'
world and I can see opportunities for Shyla's story to come to life.
Trouble is, when I wake up and try to put into words the colours
and the sounds of the parched dry landscape I struggle to make
it as real as it has been in my head. Still, the process of creating is
satisfying enough and hopefully some of it will eventually make
its way onto paper.

I can visualise my book covers, the blurb on the back, the
reviews citing my writing as being 'a fresh voice in a landscape of
homogenised teenage literature'. My drawings 'vivid and quirky'.
I will travel the world doing book signings and be recognised as
one of the great graphic novelists of my generation.

Unfortunately, my slumbering was rudely disrupted by the
sound of Kveta's television in the next room. She seems to need

the television on constantly. The theme tune of *Keeping up with the Kardashians* blared out forcing me out of bed and into the shower.

Stella would be up and about, catching up on the week's post, checking her emails and reading the *Irish Times* magazine. I knew if I timed it right I could get Stella to give me a lift to Nora's on her way to the gym. Perhaps it would be the right time to subtly mention the photograph. I doubted it though, as Stella likes to play her Spotify playlist loudly in the car and sing along to Beyoncé, Coldplay or Snow Patrol or The Script. These are her guilty pleasure bands. If someone was to ask what music she liked, she'd lie and say Kanye, Royal Blood and Kasabian. I've tried to find the right moment to ask Nora about it. Trouble is, Nora has become even more withdrawn and difficult than normal. She seems to be worried about something and I am sure I saw tears well up in her weary eyes as she stroked Maisie, the Rottweiler with no bite, last week. It was as if something had upset her. She was anxious and jumpy and when the postman rattled the letter box she blanched printer paper white.

When I arrived at Nora's I was surprised to find the garden empty. Normally I am greeted by several dogs and the odd cat wrapping itself around my legs, looking for some attention. The hutches were all stacked as normal and the rabbits seemed happy enough. Muted barking from inside the house suggested that Nora had taken the dogs in.

I tried the back door, which was usually left open for me to let myself in, only to find it locked. I knocked and heard the dogs scurry towards the door and bark in welcome. I could picture Maisie hurtling herself against the back door and sure enough within a minute I heard the thump of a heavy dog throwing itself against the other side of the wooden door. Nora didn't appear and I was filled with dread. Perhaps she had taken sick in the night or had fallen over and was lying in a pool of blood. With fresh urgency I banged on the door, and called out, 'Nora, Nora!'

'Steady on, I'm coming,' I heard from within the hallway.

I suddenly felt a bit stupid for letting my imagination run away with me.

'What's the panic?' asked Nora as she opened the door.

'It's just that the door is usually left unlocked and the dogs aren't in the garden so I thought something might have happened to you.' I hung up my hoodie on the back of the wooden door and gave the dogs a ruffle and a scratch in response to their barking and jumping around.

'Just didn't want snoopers, snooping around again,' said Nora.

'What snoopers?' I asked, wondering if Nora had finally lost all sense of reason.

'Council snoopers, that's who. Came around here, asking about permits and whatnot. Said I was breaking regulations left, right and centre.' She picked up a sheaf of papers from the kitchen counter, thrusting them towards me. 'When Rosie barked at him he walked straight into the blue tits' nest hanging on the washing line and frightened the poor wee birds half to death. A big bully of a man, he was. Said this lot would have to go. Go where, I said, and he said the city dump was his best suggestion. The cheek of him,' Nora finished, her breath short and laboured.

I gave the papers a quick look over. They seemed like council official notifications of some sort but I knew I would need to sit down and read through them carefully.

Nora was obviously shaken. Her hands trembled as she poured tea into her cup and she looked even more dishevelled than normal.

'Here, let me do that,' I offered, taking the teapot from Nora. 'We'll sit down and look at the letters and see what they want and work out what we can do about it,' I added, sounding way more confident and grown up than I felt.

Nora sighed and did as I said, almost meek in her demeanour, as if all the bluster and fight had been knocked out of her.

Chapter 15

Rugby shirts and humping frogs

Monday 7.20pm

Food: one ham bap, one shortbread biscuit, one apple square, pasta bake, wedges, salad, jambon.

Lonely Girl Blog

Bad weekend. Went with Matt to see Ollie. Gruesome. His face is a mess —seven shades of green, blue and yellow. His eyeball is blood red and his nose looks like someone has stamped on it, which of course they could well have done. His bottom lip is split open and he had to have five stitches in it. It looks like his mum has sewn it together with two pieces of black thread looped and tied into a knot.

We told him that he didn't look too bad but I don't think he believed us. His mum said we weren't to stay too long as she wanted him to rest. She hung around on the landing as if frightened to let him out of her sight.

Matt wanted to know if Ollie knew the fellas who'd done it but he just shrugged. They thought he was a Protestant because he was wearing his Ireland rugby top. I almost asked how come, but managed to keep the words clamped in my mouth and processed the sick rationale: if you play rugby you're more likely to be Protestant – even if your chosen team is Ireland. Guess you have to be born and bred Northern Irish to go along with that reasoning.

Matt explained to me on the way home that Ollie's dad is from a Protestant family while his mum is a Catholic, so they have what he called a 'mixed marriage'. This was supposed to explain everything but just confused me even more. I thought that if he was representative of both communities then he would be safer from all the sectarian stuff – apparently not, it just makes him more threatened by both sides.

We told Ollie about school and how Mrs Dornan had taken a psycho in English when no one had bothered to learn their designated verse of *Death of a Naturalist*. Seamy Nelson tried to bluff his way through it, making it up as he went along. He kept saying random sentences like 'gush and throttle, the frog humped around', and Mrs Dornan blew a gasket. It was well entertaining, except we're all now expected to learn twice as many lines. I nearly cried with laughter at the time though and Jessica Bailey was laughing so much that she snorted in a highly unattractive way.

I felt kind of funny seeing Ollie. A bit sick and nervous. His poor face looked so sore that I would've liked to have taken his hand in mine and held it just for a minute, but knew better than to embarrass him like that. He seemed embarrassed enough with us being there and seeing him in such a state. His bedroom was covered in rugby posters and I wondered if what had happened made him feel differently about being a rugby supporter. Silly thought really, but it was just that when I saw his rugby top slung over his chair it made me feel sad. It was as if rugby would be forever tarnished.

Still, I'm glad I went to visit him.

Chapter 16

Dinner at Matt's and Beauty fascists

Tara
Wednesday 9.26pm

Food devoured: muesli, soy chocolate shake, chocolate raisins x one bag, salad bap, one apple, lasagne, garlic bread, sautéed potatoes and green salad, apple tart with ice cream and one mandarin orange.

Lonely Girl Blog

Had dinner at Matt's. Sat staring out of his bedroom window for ages just listening to the rain as it drummed a steady rhythm against the window pane. The street below was washed slate grey and I could see people scurrying along to try to find shelter. I *love* being invited to Matt's house for tea. The smell of lasagne and garlic bread wafted up the stairs making me hangry. You would have thought I was starved, which of course I practically am at home, especially when Stella is on shopping duty coz then the trolley is full of GI foods, whatever that means.

Dinner at Matt's is always delish, proper food, fattening and satisfying followed by apple crumble and custard or sponge cake with raspberry jam middle which Rae calls roly-poly.

I was sitting looking at the world going about its business when Matt said, 'So do you think Jessica will be going to watch the Gaelic match?' He did this without taking his eyes of the video game. He was playing Crash Bandicoot and was two hundred points from the final level.

I turned from the window leaving a smudged imprint from where I had pushed my snubby nose against the cool pane of glass. 'Since when have any of the Jessica crowd gone to Gaelic matches?' I asked reasonably. It is unheard off. They don't *do* sport. There's probably some sort of rule that says if you want to be part of the Jessica crowd you must never risk having a Sweaty Betty body or a Dirty Gertie face.

Anyway, he says, 'Well if you asked them they might come.'

And I say, 'Yeah, sure I'm just going to wander up to them and say do you fancy hanging about up at the freezing cold, windswept Gaelic pitches to watch Matt running around a muddy field chasing a ball. As if.'

Sometimes Matt is so deluded on so many levels.

Matt put the PlayStation handset down. 'Damn, I missed the next level. Come on, let's go see if the dinner's ready.'

Ate so much I had trouble leaving the table, so I discreetly opened the top button on my jeans and remained sitting talking to Matt's parents Rae and Ray – I know, hilarious – about school, SATs and GCSE choices. Matt's little brother Donal kept rocking back and forth while we were chatting. He has autism. Matt says he's a spacer but he says it with affection. They all dote on him. He sort of bosses everyone about but in a quiet way.

After dinner Rae was working so we had to keep an eye on Donal. Rae works as a doula – a birthing partner is how she describes it. Matt says it's weird living in a house where pregnant women are always wobbling about looking like they are about to drop – his description not mine.

Sometimes Rae has to race out in the middle of the night to help deliver a baby and then Matt has to help get Donal ready for school. Matt says he throws a psycho when Rae isn't there as he hates any change to his routine, so it takes both him and his dad to wash and dress him and give him some breakfast.

Matt has a scar on his arm where Donal bit him once taking a chunk of his flesh out with his teeth. Matt says he doesn't mind though coz Donal has 'heightened awareness'. Everyday happenings terrify him if they vary at all. He feels things like a million times more than us and if he hears a noise which is unfamiliar he literally goes into spasms of terror.

Most of the time, though, he seems happy.

He has a bit of a weird American accent. Matt says its coz he likes to watch Disney movies over and over again. His school bus picks him up at the house and takes him to the special school across town. Matt says his mum and dad worry about how Donal will cope when he is older.

We watched *Toy Story* with him, twice.

Monday 8.08pm

Food snacked on: Granola and crunchy nut cornflakes – all mixed together, one pear, one jammy dodger, one packet of ready salted crisps (why are they called ready salted and not just salted?), Kveta's stew/goulash thingy.

Lonely Girl Blog

Phone call with Virtual Mother:

VM: 'Tara, stop being such a baby. It's a social occasion, we will have our hair and make-up done for us, we will arrive in a smart, chauffeur-driven car, you go in, you nibble on some canapés, you sip some champagne, and make small talk. What is so bloody difficult?'

I could just picture Stella rolling her eyes in exasperation and throwing her hands upwards as if to ask the gods above for inspiration.

Me: 'Mum, *firstly* I won't *like* the food, secondly I am *fourteen* and I am not *legally* allowed to drink champagne, and thirdly I won't *know anyone to talk to*!' I folded my arms and scowled (she was on speaker phone). Stella could go on all day but there is no way I am going to the stupid magazine party.

Saturday 8.08pm

Tortured at the hands of beauty fascists. Sat in très plush hotel room having my hair twisted and curled into long burnished golden ringlets by a short, squat, Scottish guy called Rabbie, while my foot rested on the knee of Nancy, one of a team of beauty technicians, as they called themselves, who was painting my nails bright fuchsia pink. Another make-up artist tested swabs of foundation shades on my freckly cheek to find an exact skin-tone match. In an adjoining room Stella was undergoing the same transformation but was obviously loving it, as I could hear her boasting to Joni on her phone that she was being transformed by the best in the business.

'Ow!' I said as Rabbie twisted my hair a tad too enthusiastically.

'Sorry,' he said in his rough, gravelly accent, 'we all have to suffer for our beauty.' Heard that one before and it didn't end prettily.

I scowled; bad enough that I had been forced to go to the stupid party without having to be mutilated in the name of titillation beforehand.

This is what happened at the party:

Never seen so many strange people all in the one place. I could divide the room into three groups:

1. Those who strived to try to look quirky and different, like the fella with a blue Mohican who was wearing a sort of kilt;
2. The cluster of thin, brown and blonde-haired girls who all looked like variations of the same girl; and then
3. The magazine executive types, my mother included, who was wearing a trendy but professional-looking get up and spoke louder and higher than everyone else.

'Tara, come and meet Jago, he's a complete hoot,' Stella said as she literally dragged me off to meet the infamous Jago; turns out he is the one with the blue hair and wearing the kilt. She hissed in my ear. 'For God's sake smile and pretend to be enjoying yourself.'

I did my daughterly duty to rearrange my face into a version of a smile.

'Hello, nice to meet you,' I said.

'You were completely right, Stella, she could be a cover girl any time soon. Give it a couple of years, sweetie, and we will have you walking the catwalks of Milan.' He beamed at me as if he had just promised to take me to Disneyland.

On the upside, for once I didn't feel too tall. Normally I avoid standing too close to anyone in school for fear of dwarfing them and making myself look even more ginormous, but scanning the room I realised that the average height must have been six foot. All the girls were leggy and sleek, like giraffes stalking around the room while fluttering their impossibly long and obviously false eyelashes. Stella says the next big thing is eyelash transplants – from ostriches!

Later that night in Stella's little apartment, as we sat side by side removing our make-up, she turned to me and said, 'Thanks for coming, honey, it helped to have you at my side. I was so nervous all week.'

I wiped away all traces of the evening's sparkly gloop, processing Stella's words. It had never occurred to me that Stella might just need my support sometimes.

So much homework to do: four pages of maths, a history essay on the plantation and need to study for tomorrow's French oral test.

Stella

Tara shimmers in her gown like a newly hatched mermaid. She doesn't yet know how to carry her beauty and own the power it bestows on her, but with the right guidance, she'll learn. I'm watching everyone, enjoying the moment when Lavinia Macintosh sidles up beside me and murmurs, 'It must be irksome to have a pretty daughter – everyone compliments her and overlooks the mama bear.' It takes all my willpower not to pour my espresso martini over her platinum-dyed hair. Does anyone think that Beyoncé feels jealous of Blue Ivy? How ridiculous. Tara is my greatest accomplishment and I revel in her successes. Lavinia is a dried-up old clam with no hope of producing her own beautiful child.

We have our photographs taken against a wall of pink and red peonies. Everyone looks beautiful and Tara beams at me. The music swells around us and the mood is fun and playful. Someone is wearing a Venetian mask and a top hat. There's a fire eater standing on a table while an acrobat is swinging above our heads. They are serving gin cocktails in vintage china teacups with tiny metallic macaroons on the side of the saucers. Tara looks at me with her eyes wide and bright. It's as if for the first time she sees the magic in my world. I'm so happy that she agreed to come with me tonight. Sure, I can't get rat-faced drunk or have a cheeky cigarette, but I'd trade every drunken night for one magical night with my girl. Once the awkward teen years pass, we'll be able to be friends. I know I'll always be her mother but I'm certain we'll never have the iceberg of mistrust and dislike between us that I have endured with my own mother.

The next morning Tara wakes and catches me watching her. It's so rare that she agrees to sleep with me these days, that I practically jumped up and down when she suggested we slept in the double bed after the party. My Dublin apartment is tiny, no bigger than a studio, so it made sense to bunker down together. We chatted and giggled about the night into the small hours of the morning, eventually falling to sleep cuddled up together. I know it can't last, we'll be sniping at each other by the time we hit the motorway home, but for now I'm enjoying the moment.

Chapter 17

How my mother ruined my life: part two

Stella

Honoured and delighted to be asked to give a little motivational career talk at Tara's school. I couldn't possibly have allowed my parents anywhere near my school. The shame would have been too much. Thankfully, if anyone understands teens and their emotional hang-ups it's me. They are my audience, after all. When Ms Ambrose called inviting me along, I could hardly say no. I'm sure they don't have too many international journalists on the parents' mailing list. My experience in life and work is extensive and it is only fair that I pass it on. I've read Sheryl Sandberg's *Lean In*. Well, I've read the blurb. I understand that women have to take a seat at the table and to make their voices heard. I have Beyoncé's 'Lemonade' on my Spotify most-played list. This qualifies me to be a female leader in my field. I shall go to the school and make my mark. No point telling Tara in advance. I'm sure she'd come up with a million reasons why I shouldn't do it. She'd get herself all stressed and worked up in that way she does. Better for me to rock on up there and deliver my speech like it's a Ted Talk. She'll thank me later. I know she will.

Tara

Food swallowed: one coconut yogurt, one pancake, one croissant with raspberry jam, one kiwi, one Mars bar, one mouldy Creme Egg half-

eaten, one slice of pizza from school canteen, one can of club orange, one ham sandwich, two slices of toast with Nutella.

Lonely Girl Blog

Mort. i. fi. cation. How could she? She didn't even tell me. Said it was to be a surprise. I am the laughing stock of the entire year 9s and 10s. How can I ever live this down? Perhaps we will move again and I can start over. It's the only solution.

I was sitting in the assembly hall patiently listening to Ronan McAuley's dad give a career talk on working in sales and marketing. He talked about incentives, customer relations, building up a portfolio of contacts, being a 'people' person. Just as I tried to stifle a yawn, I saw her. Just left of stage standing in her knee-high patent boots with a short tartan kilt, it was none other than Stella, my so-called mother. Obviously waiting to give her spiel about working in journalism. I couldn't bear to hear it. Before she had a chance to take to the stage I stood up, pretended I needed to urgently get to the bathroom and shuffled my way down the rows of year 9s and 10s, all sitting about to witness my social demise in the form of my mother subjecting me to ritual humiliation.

HOW COULD SHE?

Chapter 18

Pleasantly surprised in Chemistry

Tuesday 6.34pm
Tara

Food consumed: One ham and cheese bap, a banana, Innocent smoothie, cup of hot water with lemon, apple pastry square, one hotdog, an apple, pasta bake.

Lonely Girl Blog

After a sleepless night of torment and torturous images of my complete ruination, I decided that the only way to ride out the storm would be to pretend I don't exist. It has worked in the past – when I have been the butt of some joke in primary school in London or later when I arrived as the new girl in Belfast, I sussed out that if I said nothing and kept my head down, people eventually failed to notice me.

It was double Chemistry first thing. I slouched down in my chair trying to will myself to disappear or just blend into obscurity.

This is what we had to copy down from the whiteboard:

'Understand how the reactivity series of metals can be determined by considering their reaction with oxygen, water and acid, and learn how to use the reactivity series to make predictions about other reactions.'

I decided I would lose myself in the class and try to not let Stella and her public appearance at school assembly bother me anymore. God, my face is still flushed scarlet hot from the memory. Even sitting in Chemistry while trying to remain focused and present, every now and then scalding, angry tears threatened to spill out of my eyes, completing the humiliation. I couldn't let anyone see how much it had upset me. They are like rabid dogs – don't let them smell your fear. If they sense my shame the teasing will be even worse.

Yesterday had passed in a blur. No one had dared mention Stella to me. I had managed to get through the last two periods of the day before rushing home, whereupon I locked myself into my room, raging between anger and despair. Of course, Stella failed to see the problem. She told me to stop being so melodramatic, that everyone had applauded and some of the girls and even a couple of boys had asked lots of questions at the end of the session. I was supposed to be delighted that she had reorganised her schedule to be in Belfast on a Dublin day.

Miss Winston told us to open our textbooks at page fifty-four. Just as I bent down to take my book out of my Kanken backpack, Freya slipped a note onto my desk.

I opened my textbook and hid the note on my jittering knee.

So it begins, I thought, the nasty notes, the jibes and mocking. But when I unfolded the piece of file paper I was surprised to read:

'We are all meeting up at Jess's house on the last Friday of term for party celebrations! Do you want to come? Freya x'

I turned to look at Freya, certain she would be smirking at me as if to say, 'did you really think I meant it?'

But Freya just smiled at me, a real, genuine smile, her dark glossy hair falling down over her sweetheart-shaped face as she nodded, encouraging me to say yes.

What to do? I smiled back, tentatively. I didn't want Freya thinking I was desperate for a friend. But how could I not respond? Maybe Freya wasn't so bad after all.

Stella

Instagram followers: 745
Twitter followers: 3,299

Facebook friends: 365
Weight: 9 stone 8 pounds
Mood on a score of 1–10: 3

My daughter did not appreciate my career talk. I am under house arrest. No drinking, no shenanigans with Dylan, no shopping trips. I must do better. Going forward I will resolve to learn how to meditate and to do proper yoga. I will no longer watch *Love Island* or *Keeping Up With the Kardashians*.

My neck is aching from trying to look like I'm reading an actual book. Tara is on the floor drawing her adorable little comic. We are endeavouring to have some family time without actually doing anything, from what I can tell.

'Water?' I ask to break the gloom.

'No, I'm fine.' She doesn't look up from her sketching. I'm being punished. It's all I can do not to lie on the floor beside her and beg for forgiveness. I hate it when Tara is cross; it's like being fifteen again and dealing with my mother's disapproval. I get off the sofa to go in search of water as something to do. The highlight of my Sunday has been chugging down Evian. What's a girl to do?

I look out across the back garden and decide that I must organise a gardener. The lawn is beginning to look bedraggled. The last time it had some proper attention was when we bought the house. The clouds are hanging dark and low. I'd almost forgotten how desperate Belfast summers are.

Tara
Friday 7.08pm

Food enjoyed: Weetos with milk, packet of chocolate raisins, can of 7up, chicken tikka, salad bap, lamb curry and rice.

Lonely Girl Blog

Last day of term and a big night out looms.

Mrs Dornan was droning on about poetry today. 'A poem shouldn't necessarily mean something – it should just be. Does anyone agree with that statement?' she asked.

I kept my head down. The rule is don't make eye contact and don't volunteer an answer.

We were reading Carol Ann Duffy's poem about a boy stealing a snowman. I really like the poem. I can visualise the teenager on his night-time stealing spree and enjoy the sense of ridiculousness of him stealing something as stupid as a snowman. And it reminded me of living in Leeds when I was little.

There was one morning when we woke to find that we were literally snowed in. At least a metre of snow had fallen overnight. Stella had phoned her newspaper office to say she'd have to work from home, she would write about the snow and the lack of snowploughs in the district and email it in. The two of us set about having a snow day. We built a snowman as proud and majestic as the one in the poem.

'Tara, can you tell us what the poet wants us to feel for the speaker?' Mrs Dornan asked, dragging me back out of my daydream.

'She wants us to feel sorry for him and his lack of family and love and his need to be part of something that he can never have.' Don't know where that came from but thankfully it seemed to do the trick.

'Yes, excellent.'

I don't really know why, but I know exactly how the boy in the poem feels.

Later I lay on my bed thinking about the snowman thief and how life has somehow cheated him and his only response was to isolate himself and try to destroy all the things he so desperately wanted to have. For once I have decided not to be so hard on Stella. She had to go it alone and worked hard at her career not just for the financial rewards and the glory of a by-line but for me too, to give me comfort and security. We may not have had an extended family but we had each other.

Chapter 19

Ghostly sex noises

Wednesday 6.34pm
Tara

*Food scoffed since dinner: spring roll, can of Coke, coconut creams x
4, Jaffa Cakes x half a packet.*

Lonely Girl Blog

So tired. Couldn't sleep last night. Spent the evening drawing
sketches of Shyla. Changed her outfit and hair – she now
wears a sort of short wrapped-round ragged dress and her
hair is short and pixie like. Went to bed as normal, read some of
my Stephen King book *Duma* – but Reba the anger management
doll is freaking me out; don't like scary dolls in horror books since
they really work as a device. Must make a mental note to use a
doll in my next graphic novel. Scary

I must have been asleep for an hour when I was awoken by a
strange groaning and the thump, thump, thump of what I thought
was the headboard against the wall. Cringe-making sounds that
no daughter should have to hear.

Put the pillow over my head to block out the sounds when I
realised that it was Tuesday night and Stella was in Dublin. Sat up
and checked my phone – she had texted me at ten to say 'night,
night'. The sounds stopped suddenly and all was quiet.

Think we have a ghost in our house and what's worse it's a ghost who makes strange sex noises. Think I should contact Derek Acorah. Will email the programme producers.

***

The freakiest thing has happened. Stella's talk was a hit. The Jessica crowd loved her and are now being nice to me. I can't decide whether it's a good thing or a bad thing. Matt says I am reading too much into it and thinking about it all too much as usual. But that's easy for him to say since boys are known not to think too hard about anything.

He is coming with me to meet up with Freya and her friends at Jess's house on Friday. Freya was really keen for me to come and said Jess wanted me there too. She said bring a friend. I hope Matt doesn't let me down by drooling over Jess.

Am I shallow, in that I am willing to go when I used to hate everything they represented and knowing how they feel about me after their nasty comments in the toilets?

Your thoughts on this matter would be appreciated.

In response to Spoke Wheeler's query last time about Belfast I can say that it is worth a visit.

Go see the Beacon of Hope sculpture near the Waterfront Hall. Locally it is called 'Nuala with the hula', or the 'the thing with the ring'. It is a metal construction of a girl holding a big ring. It is a landmark of sorts. Also check out Cave Hill which is supposed to be the inspiration for Gulliver's Travels. If you look at the rock formation it looks like the profile of a man lying down – so it gets called Napoleon's nose. Then you can get one of the many bus tours up the Protestant Shankill and down the Catholic Falls Road. You will see lots of street art on gable walls showing scenes from their histories (note, history in NI is totally subjective) or slogans of their chosen terrorist groups.

If you get a chance, go see the Giant's Causeway in North Antrim. It is like a landscape from a science fiction book: molten rock – basalt – was forced up millions of years ago which cooled and formed into vertical hexagonal pillars as a result of an ancient volcanic eruption. Legend has it that the Irish giant Finn McCool built the causeway to walk to <u>Scotland</u> to fight his Scottish counterpart Benandonner. One version of the legend tells that Finn fell asleep before he got to Scotland. When he didn't arrive, the much larger Benandonner crossed the bridge looking for him. To protect Finn, his wife Oonagh laid a blanket over him so he could pretend that he was actually their baby son. When Benandonner saw the size of the 'infant', he assumed the father, Finn, must be gigantic indeed. Therefore Benandonner fled home in terror, ripping up the causeway in case he was followed by Finn.

As for the lingo, well, I was used to my mother's dialect and sayings so it wasn't too hard for me to fit in, but you may need some words translated.

Craic – good time/happening i.e. what's the craic or the craic was ninety

Gutties – trainers

Poke – ice-cream cone

Bog off – piss off

Lift – arrest, as in 'he was lifted', i.e. he was arrested. Or 'can you give us a lift', meaning can I have a ride in your car?

Melter – someone who is annoying

Steek – chav

Scundered – embarrassed

Eejit – is an idiot

Buck eejit – a really stupid idiot

Sound, class, stickin' out – all positives as in 'that's good'

Hope this helps.

Chapter 20

An unwelcome kiss

Tara
Saturday 12.40pm

Food: toast and peanut butter, tea, chocolate buttons, can of Coke, melon slices, a mango, strawberry yogurt, salad and wedges, Doritos.

Lonely Girl Blog

Cannot believe what has happened. Went to Jessica Bailey's house with Matt and Ollie. Matt obviously delighted to have a chance of talking to Jessica; he claimed he might even ask her out. Ollie and I didn't think he'd be brave enough. Anyway, this is what happened:

For once I was glad to have access to Stella's vast walk-in wardrobe. I wasn't going to transform myself but I wanted to at least look like I had made an effort. Though part of me hated myself for caring what they thought of how I looked. It's the conundrum facing every modern feminist.

I pulled out a lime green T-shirt with a slashed neck – no, too bright. A blue-and-yellow top with a strange geometric print was rejected as too gaudy. Next, I pulled out a sheer black blouse with a ruffled collar – too see-through.

It was half an hour later before I was able to stand in front of Stella's full-length mirror, complete with fairy lights, and feel comfortable in what I was wearing.

Tight, dark jeans accentuated my long skinny legs in a good way, while a long dark green tunic-style top prevented them from looking too candy-cane-like. The top had batwing sleeves and a bronze braided belt nipped it in at the waist. I slipped on a pair of Stella's bronze-coloured pumps and surveyed the image. I would have to do something with my hair but at least I looked *different*. Older. More stylish. My usual uniform of faded Twenty-One Pilots T-shirt and shapeless jeans could have a night off.

Matt had agreed to meet me here at my house so that we could walk together to Jessica's. When the doorbell rang I skipped down the stairs two at a time, shouting to Kveta that I was off out and would be back by ten thirty. Stella was out with Dylan. Opening the door I was surprised to see Ollie standing next to Matt.

'You look good,' said Ollie, grinning so widely that he looked a bit manic.

Of course I blushed. I had expected Matt to slag me off for the hasty image change but I hadn't banked on anyone complimenting me, least of all Ollie.

''s all right if Ollie comes, isn't it?' asked Matt.

I said, 'Sure, don't see why not.'

Matt had made an effort too. His normally scruffy hair had been slicked into a Mohican with hair gel and his usual jeans looked freshly laundered and ironed. He wore a checked shirt left open over a blue Duck and Cover T-shirt. I was sure that Jessica would approve. I suppose he couldn't give me any stick about my change of image since he had obviously gone to so much trouble.

The three of us set off to Jess's house not knowing what to expect. It was one thing to be invited into the inner circle of the Jessica crowd but another to know what to say once we arrived. Of course Ollie has been out with them before since he knows Freya well. His mum and Freya's mum have been best friends since school, so he is regarded as an honorary cousin.

We needn't have worried. Jessica seemed delighted to see us. She lives just off the posh Malone Road, her home a massive gated detached house surrounded by tall trees. We were stunned at how big Jess's house is. It's like a mansion or something, really grand, but still cosy and nice inside. The Jessica crowd were all there. When we walked in I was terrified that they would suddenly start laughing at my having accepted the invitation as genuine but no, they were really nice and welcoming.

The chatter and giggles of the other girls could be heard from the hallway.

'Come on through,' said Jessica, leading the way, 'my mum and dad are out so we have a free house.'

I noticed Matt's lovelorn gaze follow Jessica up the hallway. Ollie smiled at me as if to say, *what is he like …*

We entered a large square room which Jessica called the den. The other girls were all sitting on a low couch watching music videos on MTV. Pink's 'Funhouse' video was playing.

So there we were, sitting in her big living room, eating popcorn and Doritos. They were all being so nice, making us welcome and saying how cute my outfit was. Suddenly Freya pulled out a bottle of vodka from her Lipsy handbag and asked did anyone want a swig.

Matt, feeling he had to look cool in front of Jess, took the bottle and downed a good bit of it before our eyes. He began choking and spluttering and made himself look like a right eejit, not coz it was too strong, he said afterwards, just coz he tried to drink it too quickly.

Still the bottle was passed round and everyone took a sip. I put it to my lips but didn't really drink it. Ollie took it after me and I was strangely pleased that it would be his lips on the bottle rim after mine, but then he passed it on to Ella and I felt sick at the thought of her lips replacing Ollie's – very strange thought process.

The bottle was passed a few times before it became apparent that Matt was a bit pissed. He began showing off and talking in this loud but sometimes high-pitched voice and flirting with anyone, obviously to make Jessica jealous.

Then, completely unexpectedly, he leaned over and kissed me, full on the lips, with no warning. His lips were a bit wet and soft, but nice all the same. Just as he pulled away I saw Ollie watching from the other side of the room. His eyes looked kind of dark and *hurt*.

I pushed Matt off me and told him to wise up.

We went home by ten and said nothing about the whole incident but it has freaked me out completely.

What should I do? Do I ask Matt why he did something so stupid? Do I explain to Jess that it's her he really likes? And why did Ollie look so odd when he saw the kiss? Comments please.

Chapter 21

Virtual Mum to the rescue

Tara
Thursday 1.08pm

Food gorged from dinner time: hot chocolate with Minstrels, packet of Doritos, packets of Maltesers, one apple.

Lonely Girl Blog

'Mum, can I talk to you?' I said as I crawled up onto Stella's bed and lay down just like I used to do when I was little. Back then Stella was my whole world. I naively thought there was nothing my mum couldn't do and I was enthralled just to be on her radar.

Now I know different.

Now I have to put up with my mother hanging out with the likes of Dylan McKay, being papped by the local press with her toy boy in tow. The Jess crowd may have been impressed by Stella's career talk but I still have to live with the shame of knowing my mother was addressing my entire year group, advising them on their careers, while the boys sniggered about the length of her skirt. But even so, there are some problems you need to turn to your mum to help with and if she could fix this one then I would be forever grateful.

'Sure, Moonbeam, what's wrong?'

'It's Nora, Mum. She's in trouble.' As I finally said the words, tears spilled down my face. It's strange but I hadn't been aware of just how worried I was until lying here beside Stella, who despite everything could always take care of me.

An hour later we were sitting at the kitchen table drinking hot chocolate. Stella can make a mean hot chocolate. She follows a Nigella recipe that involves folding in flakes of grated milk chocolate, spiked with a little chilli powder.

'I'm sorry I didn't tell you earlier. It's just that I spent so long running away from Belfast, running away from Nora, that I couldn't just expect to turn up and make everything right.' Stella looked older than I had ever seen her. Her shoulders were slumped over and without make-up her normally polished face seemed naked and forlorn.

'When we moved back I called to see her, tried to make amends, but she was too stubborn. She wanted to see you but not me, so as a compromise she offered to let you work for her.' Stella sipped her hot drink before going on. 'When my dad died, Mum just sort of went in on herself. I had my job at the local paper to go to – it was my escape, but she just never left the house unless she absolutely had to.

'Over the years she became more and more difficult to live with. "Get on your knees and pray for forgiveness" she'd say no matter what I'd done. When I became pregnant with you I knew there would be no living with her. She said the baby would have to go. She'd get an adoption arranged through the convent, so no one need know. But there was no way I was letting anyone take my baby away.' Stella leaned forward and stroked my flushed cheek.

'She kept telling me my life was over, I had thrown away all my chances to do the things in life I had planned for. She was trying to scare me into handing you over to some nun but I was determined to prove to her and myself that when you arrived, life was only just beginning.'

I sighed. I had worked out that Nora was my gran. Besides the photo I had seen Nora's surname on the letters. It was as if my mum and everything she was talking about had happened to another person. It was difficult to reconcile the two images in my head.

'After you were born I could see that if I wanted to make a go of it I had to do it myself. So when you were just three months old I packed up our stuff and moved away and got on with life. Just me and you, and I think we did all right.'

'We did great, Mum,' I said, my heart aching with emotion, like someone had just stood on it, squashing all the love and feelings into a pulpy mess. It all made sense. How could Stella have managed to live with the fanatically religious Nora as an unmarried mother? I thought of the vast differences between Stella's and my upbringing and realised that, really, I had it easy. Stella was a pain, a disgrace at times, but she was also easy-going in a good way and she always make me feel, well, loved.

'It was hard at first. I don't know what I was thinking – a new baby to care for and hardly any money. We travelled all over – Costa Rica mainly and then the money started to run out and I realised you were going to need a proper home and some stability. I sort of had to prove to myself that I could still do all the things I had always planned to do.

'I set about flying back to the UK. We headed to England and I made some calls to my old paper. My editor Michael had some contacts in Leeds and within a week I had a job, found us a little flat to rent. I found you a great crèche and gradually I was able to make something of myself. I knew if I worked hard and worked my way up and moved with the right jobs I could do all right.'

I couldn't imagine how hard it must have been for Stella – all alone with the responsibility of a tiny baby to care for and no one to turn to. I shuddered to think that Nora had driven Stella to such despair.

Not that I don't like Nora – I do. Now I know the truth of it all I can even feel something like love for the eccentric Nora. Over the past few months we have grown close, or as close as Nora will let anyone beyond her beloved animals.

Now it looked like the council were going to shut St Francis's Animal Sanctuary down, leaving Nora distraught and her animals carted off to the RSPCA where, if they weren't rehomed within a certain period, they could be put to sleep. I could hardly bear to think about it. Every time I tried to imagine how it must feel for Nora, my stomach tightened into a knot of anxiety.

'Come on, we better get dressed and get over to Mum's,' said Stella.

I said, 'What, you're going to go and see Nora, I mean Gran?'

'Yes, we're going to sort this mess out and, whether she wants my help or not, she's going to get it.'

I smiled, a stupid big happy grin. It felt good to have my Virtual Mum take charge.

It was Stella to the rescue!

Nora was so broken and disorientated when we arrived that Mum phoned her GP. It seems that she is run down and emotionally exhausted. The doctor gave her some tablets and vitamins to help build her up and sent her to bed.

Stella and I set about feeding the animals and clearing up. The house was even worse than usual.

As we went about our jobs Mum talked, telling me all about growing up there and how wonderful Nora had been when she was younger. Life must have worn her down, Mum said. But things are going to be different now. We are here to look after Nora just like a real family should.

Stella showed me her old bedroom. It was right at the top of the house – two attic rooms knocked into one long room with a high ceiling. Old posters of some hairy rocker bands were still stuck to the walls. Stella couldn't believe how Nora had kept everything, even her old clothes which hung, dusty and neglected, in the big mahogany wardrobes. There was even a little Moses basket left at the foot of the bed, where Stella said I slept as a baby.

Stella sat down on her single bed with its pale pink candlewick bedspread and sighed. She looked sad and lost. I asked her what was wrong and she just said she wished it had been different – that

Nora had not made her feel so guilty and wrong for having me and that she could have had Nora's help and support when I was little. I felt so sorry for her, thinking of her trying to cope all alone in the world.

It seemed to be the right time to ask the question I had been avoiding all my life. 'Mum, didn't my dad want to help us?'

***

In response to the comments that came through following the Matt incident:

Diesel, I know he was trying to make Jess jealous but why did he have to inflict his lips on me to do so? Surely Jess will be put off him forever if she thinks I'm going out with him. I am not exactly the type of girl who has the power to make other girls jealous. Jessica would probably barf at the idea of having my sloppy seconds and I couldn't blame her.

Chapter 22

Peasant woman meets Irish islander

Tara

Food wolfed down: pizza with chicken and onion, wheaten bread with butter, a bar of Dairy Milk chocolate, one can of 7Up and some toast.

Lonely Girl Blog

Exciting development: heard back from the series producer of *Britain's Most Haunted*! Disappointed that Derek Acorah didn't reply personally but understand that he is probably away investigating all things ghostly. The email said that they will log my details and 'paranormal reportage' on their database and contact me should they wish to investigate further. Get this, the producer is called Paul Geist. I kid you not! Imagine if his middle initial is a T. Legendary.

Paul Geist got me thinking about all things paranormal and decided to carry out investigations of my own. Will research online to discover if anyone else has experienced ghostly sex noises. Will keep you posted.

Stella

My mum looks like she has stepped straight off the set of a wilderness documentary where she has been forced to forage for food and survive without civilisation. She looks completely feral. I can't even pretend that her clothes would have looked fashionable in the eighties. She is wearing layers – a long purple, cotton tunic full of holes with a moss-coloured knitted cardigan over the top and a plaid skirt that skims her knees. On top of her head she has a brown beret and I could swear I saw it twitch. The overall effect is peasant woman meets Irish islander from the famine days.

'Nice hat,' is all I can manage to say. I feel that I must say something about the attire. It can hardly go unnoticed.

She looks at me like she has seen a ghost, which I suppose to her I am. When I left all those years ago she wished me dead. Or at least that's how it felt to me. Now I'm standing in that same kitchen, the one where she brandished the frying pan, calling me a harlot and telling me I had brought shame upon her house.

Tuesday 2pm
Tara

Food guzzled: two bowls of Rice Krispies, one round of buttery toast, fries and burger, Kveta's goo and a bar of Whole Nut with can of Coke.

Lonely Girl Blog

Just had the Twelfth of July celebrations here. Very bizarre custom of celebrating/commemorating an ancient battle between William of Orange and King James. Lots of old men, and some younger ones too, dress up in sombre suits and bowler hats and wear orange sashes and march in the sweltering heat playing brass band type music and thumping big Lambeg drums. All very tribal. Belfast comes to a virtual standstill while this goes on.

Other news:

Stella has contacted some of the local papers, telling them about the eviction order. We are going to stage a protest. Mum says if the council want Nora moved then they are going to have to move her first! Yee haw!

We are roping Dylan in to the protest. He has just landed a small role playing Colin Farrell's younger brother in a big Hollywood film (or fil-lum as they say over here LOL) so the press will be keen to take his picture outside St Francis's Sanctuary.

Mum has given Nora a makeover and she looks so lovely. Her mad hair has been cut and tamed thanks to half a bottle of Frizz Ease and hair straighteners. Her old clothes have been binned and Mum has bought her some lovely trousers and tops from Marks and Spencer's and Next. She looks very smart and business-like, which is the image Mum says we have to go for. St Francis's has to look like a viable business concern not a doss house – Stella's words not mine.

In the spirit of this we have made a cull on all the religious iconography. Nora did protest but we promised to store the statues and holy pictures away carefully and said she can keep a few of her favourites on display. Obviously St Francis has to stay. Nora says her healing couldn't happen without his presence.

We are all working flat out to make the house comply with the council's endless list of regulations. Matt and Ollie have helped out and are painting the outside of the house and Ollie has called on his rugby team to help attack the garden. He has been so helpful and kind.

I think we have just about recovered from the awkwardness of the kiss incident at Jessica's house. Turns out Matt's conniving plan worked – he wanted to make Jess jealous and she is suddenly his text buddy and he is on her Facebook friends list. He says it's only a matter of time before she succumbs to his charms. LOL, poor Jess.

Carried out my further research on the ghostly sex noises. The world wide web is a scary place. Made the mistake of typing 'ghostly sex noises' into Google. Thankfully the parental controls made the necessary blocks or I could have been scarred for life. As it is, I have discovered that I probably have a poltergeist. My tender age of fourteen coupled with my sexual frustrations (which

I didn't know I had) along with my complex relationship with my mother are all a potent mix for a poltergeist to strike. Have discovered that the word poltergeist comes from the German words *poltern* which means to knock and *geist* which means spirit. They are usually benevolent spirits which playfully move things or cause noises such as bumping sounds.

I think I will ask Nora if I can have some of her holy water to carry out an exorcism. So spooked.

Thank you for all the support from fellow redheads, especially Pop Tart who told me of her own ginger distress stories. I will stay true to my roots. Up the reds!

Chapter 23

The smell from hell and treacherous blushing

Saturday 5.46pm
Tara

Food scoffed: French toast with maple syrup, fresh fruit salad, latte, fries and a hot dog, strawberry milkshake, Thai green curry and steamed rice.

Lonely Girl Blog

Working hard to make Nora's house more habitable. Have roped in Ollie and Matt. Could no longer politely ignore the bad smell, or the smell from hell as Matt has dubbed it. Matt and Ollie systematically lifted floorboards until we discovered the smell from hell. Turns out it was a dead budgie. Nora thought it had escaped and flown through the window but somehow it had ended up under the floorboards. Either it had a death wish or one of the many cats was responsible. Scruffy, the fat tabby did look kind of guilty.

The poor little budgie was cardboard stiff and more than a bit rancid. We gave it a decent burial but then Rosie dug it up, so Ollie put it in an old shoebox (of which Nora had several) and placed it in the skip Stella had hired to facilitate the clear-out.

Spent the last half hour of the sunshine sitting on the back doorstep, scratching Rosie behind her ears, while Ollie tackled the last of the garden. It is amazing how much we have achieved in such a short space of time.

I watched as Ollie reached across the fence to cut back an overgrown section of hedging. His strong arms are burnished to the colour of toast by the sun.

He has been so good these last weeks, checking in on Nora and volunteering to do whatever Stella thinks needs done. We have worked as a team along with Matt and Stella, clearing the house of all the piles of newspapers Nora has gathered up over the years, scrubbing down the kitchen cupboards and shining the windows until they gleamed in the late July sunlight.

It has been hard work but also fun. I can't help smiling even now, just thinking of all the banter as we carted out bin bags full of old clothes and rubbish, old blankets and pieces of carpet Nora had squirreled away, protesting that one of the animals might like to lie on it.

Stella has been ruthless.

She gave Nora the mad evil eye and told her, 'Mum, this place is a tip and if you intend to continue living here we have to make it habitable. It's your choice – either muck in and do what you can, or we leave now and let the council close you down.

'There are plenty of old people's homes you could go to but I'm sure they won't want this lot,' she said, gesturing to the pack of dogs which faithfully follow Nora everywhere.

Nora has acquiesced. She knows Stella is right but it is hard to change the habits of a lifetime.

'Well, it looks a lot better now,' said Ollie coming over to sit beside me on the step. We looked around the garden which although wasn't perfect was at least presentable. The overgrown lawn had to be scythed back before he was able to mow it and the flower beds, once a jumble of weeds and creepers, have been dug over and covered with a fresh layer of peaty topsoil. I bought some shrubs and placed some pots filled with geraniums to provide a splash of colour.

Nora was adamant that the rockery shrine is to remain, so we tidied it up and now Mary stands proudly overlooking a new orderly garden.

We have created a separate area for the animals with the hutches receiving a fresh lick of paint thanks to Matt and his friend Luke, as well as a good, thorough clean.

I sat there with Ollie's warm arm next to mine and said, 'You know, I am really grateful to you and Matt for helping us out.'

I could feel my treacherous cheeks sear red. It is ridiculous even now, after all the time we have spent together working at Nora's, I still feel weirded out and embarrassed talking to Ollie about anything other than sport or music.

He said, 'Wise up, it's been good fun. Besides, I like dogs and I wouldn't want to see these bad boys without a home,' as he playfully scratched Rosie. But then he added, 'Also all this hanging out at Nora's has given me the chance to spend some time with you.'

Of course my doubly treacherous face fired up anew.

Ollie. Big, blond, gorgeous-looking Ollie, enjoyed spending time with *me*? God, I was practically a furnace. Scorch!

Chapter 24

Tippex again and the au pair's poltergeist

Stella

Operation Save Saint Francis and Nora is under way.
I am mortified that my mother is in such a state. Her
house is not fit for purpose. The animals have taken over
and Nora is oblivious to the hygiene issues. The smell is rank,
somewhere between horse manure and bad mildew. You could
bottle it and use it has sex repellent. I'm cross that I allowed Tara
to be part of this. She has been working with Nora amongst the
dirt and the mould for weeks and I had no clue that these were
the conditions she was working in. While my relationship with
Nora may have been damaged long ago, I still feel that I am duty
bound to help her out of this squalor.

When I lived at home there was a semblance of normality.
Sure there were the forlorn-faced statues and the odd sprinkle of
holy water, but now, between the religious icons and flea ridden
animals there is barely space to sneeze.

Sunday 8.45pm
Tara

*Food enjoyed: scrambled eggs and bacon rashers, toast and tea, roast
dinner courtesy of the restaurant up the road, fish finger sandwich
with brown sauce, finished off with a Galaxy bar and Coke.*

Lonely Girl Blog

Conversation had today with VM:
   Me: 'Mum.'
   VM: 'Mmm?'
   Me: 'There has been something bothering me.'
   VM: 'What is it, honey?'
   Me: 'It's silly, but I just remember overhearing you chatting to Elise and Joni one night, about getting pregnant when you were so young, and you were talking about typos and making errors on your blank sheet of paper and how if it happened to me you would give me a bottle of Tippex to get rid of the mistake.

'Do you really think of me as a mistake? And what did you mean by giving me a bottle of Tippex?'

VM: 'Oh, sweetie, come here. I simply meant that we can all make wrong choices in life and, believe me, I wasn't referring to you as a mistake or a wrong choice – it's complicated. I meant that if you had a baby to the wrong man – the man you weren't meant to spend the rest of your life with – that I would help you find the *one*. Help you find your way in life. I would be there to help you and guide you and support you.'

I snuggled down into my mum's arms, satisfied. I think.

Stella

Traumatised. Poor Tara overheard me talking to the girls and has come away with some ridiculous idea that she was unwanted. She was rambling on about blotted copybooks and Tippex.

How could I have been so careless to say anything to suggest such a thing. I have never explained to Elise and Joni that getting pregnant was actually the best thing that ever happened to me. They wouldn't understand. They are still resentful of their bourgeois lives, married to Bill the banker and Tommy the software designer. Their lives have been put on hold by their husbands, but it has been much easier for them to think that it was a result of having children. Tara never stopped me doing anything. I don't mean that in a selfish 'my child will fit in with my life' kind of way. No, Tara gave me the confidence and drive to make sure I did everything in life that I ever wanted to.

When Joni and Elise became pregnant they fell neatly into the stay-at-home brigade for the first six months to a year. I get it. Who wouldn't want to be cocooned with their baby in those early days? The difference for me and Tara was that I had no one supporting me. The massive irony of this is that Tara made everything possible. I could be who I wanted to be because I had to be the best version of me for her.

Tara
Lonely Girl Blog

Planning to carry out the exorcism tonight. Asked Nora for holy water and she was delighted, thinking I have experienced some sort of religious conversion. Her face cracked into a wide smile and she said, 'My child, you have truly come home.' LOL! She gave me a plastic bottle shaped like Our Lady with a blue crown on her head, which is actually the bottle lid. The water has come all the way from a holy shrine in Lourdes where Our Lady appeared to a young girl called Bernadette. Hopefully this will make it extra potent when it comes to casting out the poltergeist. Have told Matt and he said he will video the proceedings for Derek Acorah to use on the show.

Friday 10.10am

Food consumed: toast with peanut butter, one orange and a cup of herbal tea with Jaffa Cake.

Lonely Girl Blog

Picture the scene: closed my bedroom curtains and lit some of Stella's expensive Jo Malone scented candles. Matt set up his phone on video mode to record the proceedings. All was quiet.

I blessed myself the way I see Nora do when she is about to pray and called on the poltergeist to show himself (don't know why but think it is a male spirit).

Walked around the room in clockwise circles, sprinkling the holy water when suddenly we could hear the theme tune for *The X Factor* blast out from Kveta's room. Very strange since it isn't X Factor time of year. Scared the bejasus out of us both but at least we have evidence to send to Paul Geist and Derek Acorah.

We now believe that the poltergeist has originated from Kveta. She is clearly sexually frustrated and lonesome.

Chapter 25

Bowled over

Saturday 11.02am

Food guzzled: toast and boiled egg, banana, mandarin orange, salad and fries, steak and salad with garlic potatoes, ice cream.

Lonely Girl Blog

My life is over. Completely over. Yet again.

Went bowling with the Jessica crowd. Discovered that in almost any given social situation I end up being laughed at.

This is what happened:

Friday night had been designated bowling night. The Jessica crowd had kindly extended their invite to me, Matt and Ollie.

Before we went I said to Matt, 'Please tell me that Jess knows we are not going out together.' I tried not to whine as I said it but it really was important to address the issue before we were all together again.

'Cool your wellies, it was only a kiss, hardly a commitment service,' said Matt flicking a piece of chewed rolled-up paper at the back of Ollie's head.

Met them at the bowling alley. Jessica gave me a hug in welcome. 'Glad you came,' she said, like we were old friends.

Freya shimmied up on the bench to make room for me to sit next to her while I put on my bowling shoes. 'It's a nightmare wearing these hideous things,' said Freya, unsticking her hair from her lip gloss. I nearly said something about them looking better than her Uggs but managed to refrain. No point making sartorial commentary when I am trying to be part of the cool crowd. Some things you just have to put up with.

Later when the girls' score was well down on the boys', Ollie demonstrated his bowling technique. 'Extend your arm backwards, bend your knee, follow through smoothly and let it go,' he instructed. I have to admit I was rather enjoying the attention. He was speaking directly to me. I tried not to let the fact that I had the worst score bother me and just sat there as if he and I were the only two present.

Sure, I had missed the pins completely on both turns, but at least it meant that Ollie was standing close enough for me to see the tiny brown mole behind his ear and have his hand directing my arm in a demonstration of the perfect way to bowl.

So when my turn came around, I lifted the heavy pink bowling ball and took my position at the lane.

'Come on, Tara, you can do it,' shouted Jess.

'Right. Extend. Bend. Throw,' Ollie said softly behind me. I could feel his breath on my neck.

The girls were watching intently, willing me to hit something at least. Freya had her phone out to video the shot.

I braced herself, drew my arm back and took three running steps up to the lane. On the third step I went to release the bowling ball only to find it stuck firmly on my finger, jammed against the silver ring I had put on at the last minute in an effort to look more girly.

I went down in a crash, my face slamming against the highly polished wooden floor, and heard an unmerciful crack as my wrist bone snapped like a twig being stepped on.

Bad enough to be so crap at bowling as to not hit any pins but, in an effort to impress Ollie, I had thrown my whole self, heart, soul and dignity into striking the perfect roll only to make a complete ass of myself.

Mortification heightened as the manager insisted on phoning an ambulance. Ollie, Matt and Freya followed me to the hospital in a taxi. The rest of the crowd ran to tell Stella what had happened. Oh, the drama of it all.

Ollie was really nice, though, he held my hand – my good hand – while the doctor strapped me up.

The on-duty doctor said it was the scaphoid bone and that I was unlucky since it takes longer to heal. I will have a cast on for nine weeks, which means I will have to abandon my timeline for finishing the Cave Dwellers, I won't be able to help out as much with the shelter, and it's not even as if I can have excuses for falling behind at school since we are on our holidays. Typing this very slowly with my left hand.

Got to keep a copy of my X-ray as a souvenir, though.

Of course, it was a Friday night so Stella was out partying with Dylan and her pals. Kveta had to come to the hospital in her place. Stella later claimed to feel horrified at not being there for me but I figure she wouldn't have known what to do anyhow. Stella has a history of overreacting when I hurt or injure myself.

Once when I was in primary school, Jackson Hurlington threw a marble so hard at my head, that I had to have an X-ray. The marble left an egg-sized lump on my forehead. When Stella arrived at the school to take me to hospital she took one look at the lump and promptly threw up all over her mink-coloured suede boots.

Freya captured the whole bowling alley thing on her phone and apparently it is on YouTube for all to see and hear; the cracking sound my wrist made as it snapped is legendary.

God knows what Stella would have done if she had actually heard the crack of my wrist bone. Better tell her not to look at the YouTube video.

Stella

My baby girl has been injured. Her wrist snapped under the weight of a stupid bowling ball. I feel like I could smash that bowl to smithereens. No one hurts my girl and gets away with it. I should sue the bowling alley. There should be warnings against fractures. I swear I am never letting that girl out unsupervised again. Why does no one warn you that when you have a child they can injure themselves, and that their pain is your pain, only magnified?

Chapter 26

An interesting proposal

Monday 5.02am

Food devoured: Weetabix with soy milk, grapes, apple, chocolate-covered raisins, hotdog, sweet potato with Kveta's green soup.

Dear Lonely Girl,

Let me introduce myself. I am Caroline Houston, the editor of *Kiss* magazine, Northern Ireland's leading teen periodical. Our agenda is to unearth new talent and to provide a platform for previously unpublished writers, to reach a wider audience.

Your 'Lonely Girl' blog has come to my attention and I would like to invite you to be a regular contributor to *Kiss*.

I recognise that your voice is one which would appeal to our savvy readership and we would like to tap into that element of culture in the north of Ireland.

I would be grateful if you could meet with me to discuss this proposal further.

Best regards,

Caroline Houston.

Editor in chief,

Kiss x

Very exciting happening has occurred. The above email arrived in my inbox and I am beside myself with, well, something closer to glee and excitement than trepidation and fear, though those two are not far behind.

A real magazine wants to publish my blog, my mad, sometimes incoherent ramblings. My opinions on school, Matt, Ollie, the Jessica crowd and my mother?

I have been torn between excitement and exhilaration and then sheer terror. People would see my words in print, they would be reading my thoughts. Sure, the blog is public. Anyone who stumbles across it can read it and I have been receiving hundreds of hits of late. It has somehow built up quite a following, but it doesn't feel so *exposed*. While I am tapping away on the keyboard in my own private bedroom it feels like I am, well, talking to a discreet, good friend, not the whole wide world.

But still – a magazine column, my very own, actually published writing. It is almost too good to be true, and then I had the crashing realisation of how I have portrayed Stella. The things I have criticised her for. Silly things which were fine confined to my own private world, but how would I feel, or more to the point how would Stella feel to have such things made public and in a rival magazine to boot?

What to do?

Chapter 27

Reclusive au pair and her criminal boyfriend

Tara
Wednesday 3.09pm

Food eaten: oranges, Rice Krispies, cheese sandwiches, one KitKat, one packet of salt and vinegar crisps, pasta and salad.

Oh, the drama. I am an accessory. I am at risk in my own home. I am sleeping with a knife under my pillow.

Turns out Kveta stayed in her room so much because she was hiding her boyfriend, Petar.

Apparently he arrived three months ago from his hometown of Ilok in Croatia. He has been living, rent free and undiscovered in Kveta's room, only coming out at night time for fear of being found and deported back to Ilok. It explains why she always had the television on with the volume turned up – so we wouldn't hear them speaking.

Just in case I am ever required to make a police statement on the events, this is what happened:

It was a hot, muggy July night and I couldn't sleep. The events of the past few weeks were whirling around my head like a bad movie stuck on rewind. I tossed and turned until my sheets were tangled and in exasperation I threw back the duvet and decided to go downstairs for a cold drink.

It was a Tuesday night so Stella was in Dublin. I had eaten pasta and salad with Kveta before finishing off some sketching with my left hand, so they were only rough storyboard ideas.

I had gone to bed early to read Stella's James Herbert novel *The Secret of Crickley Hall*, which, if I am truthful, was scaring the bejaysus out of me.

I tiptoed down the stairs quietly so as not to wake Kveta. The last thing I wanted was for Kveta to be moaning in the morning about not getting a good night's sleep. Of late she has become even more strange, preferring to go to bed at eight and spending as much time as possible in her room.

I could hear her snoring through the wall, a snuffly sound like Rosie sniffing around in Nora's pockets looking for a treat.

As I entered the hallway I was aware of a dim light coming from the kitchen. I froze, trying to discern if it was Kveta up, unable to sleep as well. But within an instant I was sure whoever was in there wasn't Kveta, for I could still hear Kveta's soft snoring from above.

Then, your honour, I heard the suction thump of the fridge door close. Whoever was in the kitchen was helping themselves to something out of our fridge. Their shadow was cast right across the stairway while I stood frozen. Then, just as I was about to bound back up the stairs to wake Kveta and phone the police, he moved away from the fridge and spotted me. All I could do was stand there, glued to the cold tiles of the hall floor and scream blue murder. Oh, the terror. I shall need counselling to deal with my post-traumatic stress.

When I began screaming, the fridge thief, Petar, also began screaming and Kveta ran down the stairs convinced we were being murdered.

When we calmed down, Kveta explained and pleaded with me not to turn him in to the authorities as he is here without a work permit. Seems he had some trouble with the police back home when he was caught growing marijuana in quantities large enough to be a supplier!

Despite the dubious greenhouse activities, he appears to be a very meek kind of guy. Mousey like with a beaky nose and spiked dirty blond hair. He was shaking and nervous, asking Kveta lots of questions in Croatian I couldn't understand. He was wearing Kveta's old grey towelling dressing gown, which looks like it needs a good wash, his bare legs pasty pale in the blue moonlit kitchen. Can't believe we have had a fugitive hiding out in our house. What will Stella think?

After the drama dissipated somewhat, as it would since we were all so exhausted, we agreed to sleep on it. I don't know about them but I didn't get much sleep for the rest of the night. I kept having weird dreams about the basement of Crickley Hall. That's the last time I am going to read one of Stella's books. In the dream I was climbing down the basement stairs to find Petar snoring in Kveta's arms.

I am so creeped out. I think I need to start reading less scary books. Maybe try one of Stella's romance books instead.

Think Stella needs to come home and sort out this one. I don't know what to do. On one hand I would hate to see Petar out on the streets and on the other I don't want to harbour a criminal. In the meantime, I am going to sleep with a kitchen knife under my pillow, just in case. Don't want to sound xenophobic but he is an ex-criminal and he has been hiding out in my house, eating all the chocolate cake and probably responsible for the *things that go bump in the night* noises.

Oh bum. Will have to contact Derek Acorah to inform him that the ghostly poltergeist sex noises have been explained.

Chapter 28

Nora talks

Tara
Wednesday 3.34pm

Food: Weetabix, banana milkshake, chicken soup with some crusty bread, oranges.

Lonely Girl Blog

Went to Nora's house. Stopped off at the Spar to buy supplies – tinned chicken soup, two oranges and a bottle of Lucozade. Yesterday I had called in on Nora to find her slumped over the kitchen counter coughing so violently that she had barely the strength to stand up. Her gnarled yellowing fingers clutched at the counter with all her might. I just about managed to support her weight and helped her to reach the sofa in the living room.

Later I talked Nora into going to bed and I sorted out the animals. In recent weeks we have had to refuse to take in any more animals. It was heart-breaking last week when I took a call asking for a place for two dogs. Their owner had died and the neighbour didn't know what to do with them. I sadly explained that St Francis's was full to capacity and that we were unable to commit to any new animals for the foreseeable future. Until we have complied with all the council's demands we can't take in any new animals, no matter how desperate their need is. I gave the woman the phone number for the RSPCA and said I hoped they would be able to help rehome them; trouble is I know they are likely to be split up. There are few people like Nora who would happily take on two dogs.

Nora was sitting up when I arrived. She looked a bit brighter but her skin was sallow and saggy like a deflated balloon. I think the stress of the previous month has taken its toll on her. The council officials should be held accountable for harassing an old lady who wants nothing more than to be allowed to look after some stray animals. So what if the dogs bark? You can hardly outlaw barking. And cats cannot be trained to pee in one specific place. It isn't Nora's fault that they like to use the garden next door as a litter tray. I hope (and I have to admit I have even prayed) that Nora will soon be back to her normal, grouchy self. It's funny how I miss her snarly tone and her barked-out orders.

'Surely a young girl like you has better things to do on a lovely day like this than to come and see an old woman like me,' she said today.

'I don't mind. I like coming here. Mum is in Dublin and Matt and Ollie are off training, so you have to put up with me.' I smiled at her.

I prepared a light lunch for us both, the chicken soup with some crusty bread followed by the oranges which were fresh and juicy and sweet.

'I don't know what I would have done without you these last few weeks,' said Nora, her voice weak and quiet.

'Hey, that's what families are for,' I said, clearing away the dishes and thinking how I would see to the dogs next and perhaps take them for a run later.

Then Nora said, 'I'm sure you have wondered why I didn't have more to do with you when you were growing up.'

I stood at the sink letting the warm water run over the soapy bowls, frightened to turn and meet Nora's eyes.

'Times were different then and I felt that our Stella having a baby without being married was near enough the end of the world. Cared too much about what other people thought.'

'And then when you came along I thought that perhaps I could bring you up as mine and let Stella go off and do whatever she had to do. I was probably a bit interfering to tell the truth and she wasn't one for sharing you. Said you were her child and that she'd look after you. Off she went and I was left heartbroken. I missed you both something shocking – it was like a death. The house was so quiet and empty. All I had was my dogs and God above to see me through.'

I hardly knew what to say. The normally pensive, guarded Nora had said more in those twenty minutes than she had during the entire time I've known her. If only I could make Nora and Stella see that they still need each other and that they don't have to engage in this battle of wills.

Saturday 6.05pm

Food: Crunchy Nut cornflakes, Jaffa Cakes, prawn salad wrap, orange juice, Chinese takeaway, ribs, spring rolls and rice.

Nora isn't well. Mum said the doctor has been and was concerned that she wasn't making any sense. I told Mum that's just how she is at times and it was probably just the stress of everything with the council. Now Mum isn't so sure about the protest. She said she doesn't want to take a stand only to find out that Nora truly isn't up to running the place.

How can she be so cruel? After all our hard work and all Nora's commitment to the animals. I told Mum if the St Francis is closed down it will be her fault. How can she turn Nora away now? After all we have been through, has she not learned that we need to be a family and to stick together?

I have decided that if Mum won't save St Francis then I will. I have emailed Caroline, the editor of *Kiss* magazine, to say I will meet with her to discuss the column. Yes, I know I am never ever supposed to arrange to meet up with random people off the internet but this is important. If I can use the column to promote St Francis's Sanctuary then we might just be able to persuade the council to keep it open. I will instruct Matt and Ollie to spy on me to ensure that I do not get bundled into the back of a white van and kidnapped and locked in a basement for evermore. It would serve Mum right if something happened to me. Maybe she would be sorry then for turning her back on Nora.

So with all the stuff about Nora being sick and the shelter under threat of closure and me and Stella not speaking I could hardly tell her about Petar. When Stella is in Dublin he comes out of hiding and he is actually really nice. He is a much better cook than Kveta. On Monday night we had burek – meat pie with mashed potatoes – and on Tuesday we had sausage and potato casserole. He is cooking bean stew tonight and the smell is making me hungry. He is trying to learn English and points to things for me to tell him the correct words. He watches lots of television when he is in hiding and sometimes he uses American words like 'awesome'.

Told Matt and Ollie about Petar and they think it's cool to have a fugitive hiding out in my house, but Ollie said that I could be charged with aiding and abetting a criminal and an illegal immigrant. Not sure how Brexit will affect him but we reckon it means Petar is doubly at risk of being exported back home.

Don't want to think about this as it wouldn't look good on my university application forms. Still, who said I need to go to university. I might just go travelling instead.

My hand still aches and when it becomes itchy I want to yank the cast off and give it a good scratch.

Chapter 29

Justification point

Tara
Friday 4.56pm

Food slurped up: porridge, peaches and ice cream, strawberry cheesecake, mince pie with potatoes and broccoli.

Been to *Kiss* offices. Oh my, so impressive. A real live magazine. Told the receptionist I had an appointment with the editor and she phoned up. All very slick, with huge cacti and oversized blush pink sofas in the lobby. Then Caroline showed up to bring me into her office which was at the top of the old converted Georgian style house in the university area. By the time I had climbed the four flights of stairs to reach the cramped room at the top I was slightly out of breath. Didn't seem so fancy when I realised they had no lift. Still, I suppose magazine people worry about having toned calf muscles, so all that stair climbing is vital.

It was a brightly lit office furnished with a couple of filing cabinets, a grey couch and a couple of sorry-looking succulent plants on the windowsill. The front covers of past issues of *Kiss* adorned the walls, set off in smart black picture frames.

The steady chat and buzz of the main office outside the room provided background noise. It was a real magazine office; people were taking calls and clackety clacking on their keyboards. So far, so cool.

'Can I get you a coffee or a tea or anything?' Caroline asked. Her accent, although clearly Northern Irish, was unfamiliar to me – probably somewhere like Fermanagh, I think, definitely the countryside. She was short, at least six inches shorter than me, with a neat chopped-in short bobbed hairstyle which made her look like a pixie. She was dressed in a knee-length navy pinstripe skirt teamed with a smart sharp white blouse. So much more professional looking than Stella's usual attire which can verge on the trampy. Think Toff mingled with Victoria Beckham with a dash of Alexa Chung thrown in – that's more Stella's fashion direction these days.

'No, thanks,' I replied.

Have to 'fess I was nervous and unsure of myself. Writing Lonely Girl blog has been a way of sounding off, mainly about my VM, and there I was sitting in the office of an actual magazine editor to talk about taking it one step further.

Believe it or not I was worried about hurting Stella. Even if she is annoying and selfish at times, well, truth be told all of the time, she is still my mum. The one who bandaged my hand when I fell over wearing roller skates for the first time, the one who cradled me to sleep when I had bad dreams, the one who has cared for me and loved me all my life even if it has been via remote control most of the time.

But Stella is also the one who has set about closing St Francis's Sanctuary, practically putting a death notice on the heads of all the animals there. And then there is poor Nora. How could she cope without her animals for company, and did Stella really mean it when she threatened to find a nursing home for Nora if she didn't come and live with us?

'So this blog.'

Caroline interrupted my thoughts which were hurtling along like a freight train with no brakes, desperately trying to reach justification point before it was derailed.

'You've attracted quiet a following, I hear, hundreds of readers and plenty of commentators.' Caroline leaned back on her leather swivel chair, crossing over her slender stair-climbing toned legs.

'One of our interns brought it to my attention and I have to say you can certainly write. Of course, we would need to agree an editorial line in keeping with the magazine. What do you say? Are you on board?'

Flattery is everything.

Saturday 10.45am

Food wolfed: Ulster fry and tea from the café up the road.

Turns out Caroline, my editor (do you like how I dropped that one in?), used to know my mum or at least knew *of* her. Caroline is married to Michael, my mum's first boss way back when she worked for the *Belfast News*. He was the one who set her up with the job on the sister paper in Leeds. Caroline said he often wondered how she had got on in life. She said to let her know they were asking about her.

It's funny, but Caroline looked a bit funny, wistful even, when she mentioned her name.

Haven't told Stella yet. Still waiting for the right moment; besides, the magazine is due on the stands next Friday so perhaps I would be better waiting until it is definitely in, then I can show it to her and see how she takes it.

Caroline has edited the first three blogs to make up the first column piece. I hope she doesn't stitch me up and only put in all the really bad bits about Stella. But then I can't remember writing any *good* bits about her. Oh hell, what have I done?

Matt and Ollie said they loitered around the building so long that the security guard called the police. They tried to explain that they were waiting on me but the policeman told them to clear off and if there were any break-ins they'd know who to lift.

They walked away and waited for me at the top of the road until the police had gone. Ollie offered to walk me home and Matt headed off to Gaelic training. We chatted about the Killers – his favourite band.

When I got home I found a note in my pocket: 'I think yr cool'

No name but I think it must have been Ollie. Can't believe that the other notes must have been him too. Boys are weird – why can't he just say if he likes me?

Chapter 30

On the stands

Tara
Friday 1.10pm

Food: croissant with blueberry jam.

O>M>G. It is in the magazine! I am a real, published writer. I stood gazing up at the magazine stand. There it was – *Kiss*.

The cover had a young model with glossy dark hair, her pink lips pushed tight into a Kardashian-styled pout. The straplines (I have picked the media jargon up from Stella over the years) included: *How to have a social life and study. Why he hasn't called: reasons boys don't come through, and new hair accessories to suit every style.* And beneath the headings, as ridiculous as it seemed, there was my name: *Miss Print, new columnist Tara Hunter makes her mark.*

I lifted the magazine down and flicked through looking for my piece. It was buried on page twenty-six but still, there it was in black and white with my first ever by-line. Sick with fear of what I had written and how Caroline had pasted it together, I quickly sped through the piece.

***

Since *Kiss* has been published my name has been a blaze of something – if not glory then at least notoriety. The Jessica crowd has heard about it, probably from Matt, and sent me a congratulations card. I am secretly thrilled at this and put it up on my dressing table.

I had worked myself up into a tizz at the thought of Stella reading it. Turns out I needn't have worried. She had bigger concerns. She has made a confession though and I'm afraid I can't tell you about it until I have spoken to the third party concerned. Hope to clarify all by the end of the week. I am still in shock and trying to process what I have been told.

Will give you this much information:

'Caroline Houston?' Stella asked, her voice rising an octave as if my meeting with Caroline Houston was the most unlikely event *ever*. 'Caroline who is married to Michael, who used to edit the *Belfast News*?'

'Suppose so, don't know. I didn't ask about her husband,' I replied, wondering when she would stop going on about Caroline and actually look at my column.

'Did you tell her who you were? That you're my daughter?'

'I didn't need to, she sort of worked it out from the blog,' I answered, thinking Stella was not making much sense. What did Caroline matter in all of this? Unless of course Stella thought that Caroline had some ulterior motive for printing my words.

'Your column? God, yes, wow.' At last a fitting response.

Stella looked down at the magazine to read my words. Five hundred and fifty-six words to be precise. I know, for I have counted them. Caroline has been gracious in her editing – nothing defamatory. Thank God. Wouldn't want my mother to sue me.

'Well, missy, you certainly let me have it,' said Stella closing the magazine.

Stella

We fell into a drunken smooch. Hands roaming, mouths sucking at each other's faces in that young way when kissing was still new. Michael. My first love. The memory of it still tastes sweet. The world could have been burning down, which come to think of it, in Belfast, it probably was, and I couldn't have cared less.

I did not expect Tara to be the one to bring him up in a conversation at the dinner table.

I felt my face flush with the thought of him. Tara seemed oblivious. She's still made up about her first published piece and her by-line. It appears she is a chip off the old block after all. All those times I worried that she'd become something soul destroying like an accountant or a solicitor, when really she has been honing her writing skills. What an absolute little star. The fact that I am the brunt of what she is writing about doesn't matter one bit to me. It's all copy in the end, as someone famous once said.

Chapter 31

The underpants conversation
Sunday 1.10pm

Food: scones with raspberry jam, one apple, balsamic vinegar crisps, double chocolate cookie.

Lonely Girl Blog

O>M>G!
Stella has discovered Petar. She found a pair of men's underpants in the wash and thought they belonged to Matt. She sat me down to have a discussion about 'responsible sex' with the underpants sitting on the table between us. Urgh!

The conversation went something like this:

Stella: 'There comes a time in a young woman's life when she is ready to move on to the next level of intimacy, but that does not have to mean sex.'

Me: *going bright red and looking at the underpants with suspicion*: 'Mum, we have had this chat before. Can I go and do my homework now?'

Stella: 'If you are not mature enough to have this conversation, then I don't think you are mature enough to be having sex.'

Me: *in a horrified screechy voice*: 'I am not having sex!'

Stella: 'Then how do you explain how Matt's underpants managed to find their way into our washing machine?'

Me: *sounding dense*: 'Why would Matt have put his underpants in our washing machine?'

Stella: 'Because he has obviously lost them in the heat of the moment and Kveta has picked them up along with your dirty clothes and put them in the laundry basket, I assume.'

The mention of Kveta makes me realise who the underpants must belong to. For a fleeting moment, I think of going along with her just to keep Petar's cover but can't bear the idea of my mother actually thinking that I have had sex with anyone, let alone Matt, so I am forced to come clean and blow Petar's cover.

Stella throws a complete wobbler and Kveta and Petar are ordered out of her room. After much crying (from Petar) and pleading (from me and Kveta), Stella calms down and says she will review the situation in a week's time but that Petar will have to find alternative accommodation.

Does anyone have any information on immigration rules? Ideas and thoughts would be greatly appreciated.

Note to Pop Tart: Yes, Dylan is still on the scene but he has been busy in London doing an advert for Lynx deodorant. It looks like the Colin Farrell movie has fallen through due, according to Dylan, to Brexit – they can afford Dylan but not Colin Farrell. Never mind, Stella says his career is only one personal hygiene advert away from stardom.

Stella

I have had a strange man living in my house and I had no clue. What kind of awful mother am I? Tara has been hiding it from me in an effort to protect him and Kveta. I've a good mind to sack her and send the pair of them back to whatever eastern European country they came from.

Every time I think of Tara being at risk I shudder. There are times when I look at her beautiful face and still can't quite believe that she's mine. That I alone in the world am responsible for her. Sometimes the weight of the worry is too much.

It's a beautiful day. Statistically we're bound to get one good day every summer. This year it falls on a Sunday. Tara and I are going to give Nora a hand. We have arrived at a truce, thanks in part to Tara. Nora, despite her mean and nasty demeanour, adores Tara. I know she tries to hide it but I can tell. For the first time in my life, my mother and I have something in common.

Chapter 32

Really sad, depressed, pissed off, and blue

Tara
Monday 5.00pm

Food demolished out of depression: toast with peanut butter, two scones with raspberry jam, one cup of herbal tea with a Wagon Wheel, one packet of gummy bears, fries and cheeseburger and Coke.

Lonely Girl Blog

Forced to hand Maisie and Rosie over to the man from the RSPCA. I tried to be brave and hold back the tears but it was just too much. Ollie, who was standing next to me, put his hand on my shoulder. There was nothing he could say to comfort me but it was nice knowing he was there.

We have spent weeks trying to rehouse all the animals. Freya has taken one of the beagle puppies whom she has named Marlow; Niamh's cousin, Emer, has agreed to take two cats and Anna's neighbour has given a home to two of the canaries. That leaves Gyspy the duck, the squirrel, the bats and Roxy the fox.

We are in talks with the RSPCA on how best to house the remaining animals and they are advising on the safe release of Roxy back into the wild. We have agreed on taking her to the wooded area of Shaw's Bridge, but I want to allow her to stay at the shelter for as long as possible.

One by one the animals are moving on, leaving Nora's house an empty ruin.

Nora is sick. Really, really sick, like the adverts on the television for Cancer Research sick.

Cancer, they said, in her right lung, nestled down beneath all the alveoli (we covered it in Biology), slow growing little cells, dividing and multiplying unnoticed until she began to wheeze and then cough. The doctor thought she had pneumonia but when the antibiotics didn't help he sent her for an X-ray. That's when everything changed.

She is doing better now. She knows she has been diagnosed with cancer and had surgery to remove a tumour in one of her lungs. I'm not so sure how Nora will be when she comes home from hospital, but I know that at least me and Stella will do our best to look after her.

Went to see her yesterday.

'How's my girl?' Nora asked, lying between the starched white sheets of the hospital bed.

'Good,' I said, fighting to hold back the dam of tears which have been building up for days.

Stella had told me about Nora being ill as gently as possible. She said that years of smoking had caused it but that Nora was lucky since the doctor was optimistic that he could treat it. But nothing could lessen the blow. After all those years of living in Leeds and then London with no family beyond my mother, I can't believe how cruel God is, to now threaten to take Nora away. Even though Stella said the cancer has been caught early enough, I'm not a baby; I know that it could come back and if it does it will eat away at Nora until she dies.

The nurse hovered by the end of the bed, checking the paperwork on the metal clipboard. An IV stand whirred as it dripped a clear, colourless liquid down a rubber line into Nora's veins. Someone across the ward coughed. A hacking, painful-sounding cough.

I took hold of Nora's frail hand. The skin was tissue paper thin exposing an intricate network of purple and blue veins.

'Mum said she will be in later. She has managed to persuade her editor to let her be based in Belfast for the next six weeks so she can keep an eye on both of us.' I tried to smile but my face felt all tight and strained.

'That's good. We can keep an eye on her too,' replied a tired Nora.

'Gran?'

'Yes, love?'

'Are you still sad about the shelter?'

'There's a time and place for everything, and as much as those animals needed me to give them a home, I needed them to give me bit of company. But sure look at me now – lady muck, being waited on hand and foot.' She chuckled. 'No, Tara, I'd much rather have you and your mum back in my life than all the strays in Belfast. The man at the RSPCA will make sure to do his best by them and sure isn't Skipper going to stay with us?'

'Yes, Gran, Ollie is taking him out for a walk later.'

I couldn't help smile at the thought of six-foot Ollie walking a little three-legged poodle like Skipper. He has been calling round of late even without Matt, which at first was a bit awkward for both of us. He calls at the door and says he's just passing, or that he's wondering if Nora needed Skipper walked, but gradually he has become more relaxed, as if he doesn't need an excuse to be here, and just makes himself at home.

Stella has cancelled our holiday plans to go to Portugal for a fortnight so that we can look after Nora. She is still going to some dippy music festival in Dingle but thankfully I don't have to accompany her.

Reasons to like Ollie:

1. He looks good in a clean, freshly scrubbed kind of way. He is fit in both senses of the word and is taller than me, only by an inch but it still counts.
2. He smells good all the time – kind of like chewing gum and zesty lemons, even after rugby training when he is all

sweaty he smells musty and salty and it's still nice. Don't be grossed out by this, trust me.

3. He is smart but not a smart arse i.e. he doesn't *try* to look clever like Matt.

4. He wears normal clothes – tracky bottoms and T-shirts or ordinary jeans, not super skinny tight ones, and sometimes nice check shirts open over a white T-shirt.

5. Even though he seems to like me (evidence of the random notes, his volunteering at the shelter and his ability to put up with my sometimes incoherent ramblings), he doesn't come over all weird like Matt does with Jessica. But then maybe he doesn't fancy me as much as Matt fancies Jess? Maybe no one can fancy anyone as much as Matt fancies Jess.

Stella

I throw my good Valentino rockstud handbag into the car in a temper. Why after all this time does Nora have to be sick? I have wasted years running from her. Never being able to be in the same room as the woman without wanting to hit her over the head with something. The religious statues, the praying, the hoarding, the menagerie of animals. It was torturous visiting in that cesspit of a house. And now, finally, we have found neutral ground in the form of my sweet, adorable Tara and the gods above have to rain down on us by making Nora ill. She's going to die. She's going to have a slow, horrible death and I will have to watch it. Even worse, my beautiful, kind-hearted girl will have to bear it too. I can't take it. Argh!

All the beautiful bags and shoes in the world won't help numb the emotional pain of this. My heart throbs, my head thumps and my belly aches.

Chapter 33

Sugar daddy

Tara
Tuesday 6.09pm

Food: pancakes, banana, BLT, can of 7up, yummy rice and chicken dish made by Petar.

Lonely Girl Blog

First day back at school after the summer and already my life is in chaos. Can't believe it. Just can't take it in. Where to begin? Firstly, we knew last month that Nora would need surgery and chemotherapy. She has been recovering from the surgery in hospital and when she is strong enough they will begin dripping the poison into her bloodstream to kill the cancer cells. Mum says she will be very ill, her hair will fall out and we will have to prevent her from catching infections. Her house is too damp and cold for her to live in so we have persuaded her to live with us. Kveta is going to help be her carer and we have put Petar to good use packing up and clearing out Nora's house.

As if all of this isn't bad enough, I came home from school to discover a strange man sitting in our kitchen. He looked all relaxed and chatty sitting next to Stella just like they were old friends. I dumped my blazer and school bag on the floor and just stood there, wondering what he was doing in our kitchen.

Of course, turns out he is Michael Houston. Can't imagine how there was ever anything between them though coz he is very old – at least forty-five. Probably handsome in an old-man distinguished way – greyish hair and tall and all but can't imagine him and Stella ever going out. He probably felt sorry for her having to run off with a new baby and find work all alone in Leeds with no husband or family to take care of her.

'Here she is now,' said Stella, sounding rather anxious. 'Tara, this is Michael Houston, Caroline's husband. I spoke to you about him.' She said this as if it is all perfectly reasonable.

'Do you remember I said that Michael and I used to be friends?'
Can't say I do, mother dearest, but please go on.

My heart was going a dinger, as Matt would say. Without knowing exactly why, I knew that there was something of great importance about to be announced.

'I did tell you about him.' She looked at me with these wide eyes as if imploring me, to somehow telepathically know what she is trying to say.

Then he stood up and moved towards me and said, "Tara, I'm your father.'

It was like a spoof version of Star Wars.

Ha, no, Mummy dearest, you failed to mention that he is my long-lost-never- before-mentioned father. Don't know whether to like him or hate him but can't feel anything towards him at present. I was struck numb. He sat back down and resumed playing with the milk jug as if it was somehow more important than making eye contact with me.

Michael is not only my editor's husband and my mother's former editor, but also my *father*. They had a brief relationship while my mum was his junior reporter and I became the sequel.

Put that in your magazine column Caroline Houston!

As if discovering your long-lost father isn't enough for one week, I have also found out that I have two half-sisters, Beth who is eleven and Maya who is eight. A year ago my family consisted of me and my mum. Now I have a gran, a dad and two half-sisters. Michael and his wife Caroline want me to meet their daughters. It is freaking weird! Excuse me while I hyperventilate.

Of course, I had a bit of a hissy fit. Accused him of nepotism, using the promise of the column as a ruse to trick me into meeting him. He denies any knowledge that I was the writer of the blog before I actually met Caroline. Took me a moment to process this – of course she had emailed Lonely Girl and Lonely Girl replied to her to set up the meeting. She didn't know my actual name until we met. Still suspicious. Will have to review blog security to see if she could have hacked into my computer to find out all my personal details. But then again, powers of deduction would be enough; if she knew that Stella worked for *Heart* – perhaps she has followed her career trajectory over the years. She has plenty of entries if you Google her, plus she feels compelled to broadcast every aspect of our life on Instagram.

Stella

I had no alternative but to track Michael down and break the news to him. Ta-da. Congratulations. It's a girl! You're a daddy!

Belfast is a tiny place. South Belfast is an even tinier place and the media circle within South Belfast is the size of a pizza. It was going to get even messier if I didn't deal with my mess. Not that Tara is a mess, or Michael for that matter. The mess is the fact I never ever told either of them about the existence of the other.

It wasn't easy. He was gracious and understanding. He had met Nora once so he realised that I wouldn't have found much support at home. Going it alone seemed brave at the time but now I realise it was a selfish thing to do. I kept Tara all to myself for far too long.

Chapter 34

Tara

An alternative existence
Saturday 5.09pm

Food consumed: French toast with maple syrup, a mug of tea, carrot cake, strawberry milkshake, and an apple.

Lonely Girl Blog

Woke up feeling jittery and a little bit icky. Dressed in my best outfit – skinny white jeans and a dove grey T-shirt with a navy cardigan on top for the 'family meeting'. Yikes! Desperately wanted to make a good impression, though why I was the one feeling so nervous I don't know. It's Michael who should have been the bag of nerves, since he was the one about to introduce his family to the sister they didn't know existed until a few weeks ago.

Stella thought it was best if I went alone. It would be hard enough for Michael's wife Caroline dealing with me, let alone the ex-girlfriend as well, she had said. To be truthful I was glad. I wanted to make my own impression without Stella's over-colourful personality to steal the show. Sometimes I feel that I have grown up in Stella's shadow, frightened to show too much of myself in case I come out as carbon-copy Stella. Truth is we have more in common than I am often ready to admit. We both like carrot cake, watching *ET* so many times we can recite huge chunks of the dialogue, we both love autumn walks, writing, and we have even agreed on trying to keep Gran living with us.

Now with a father to get to know I had a small buzz of excitement growing. He could fill in all the missing bits of my personality, like was he good at drawing, did he read horror books and did he like animals, and where did my red hair come from?

I unfolded the pale pink piece of paper on which I had written his address: 49 Knockway Park Road. I had found the road easily enough. It was a wide street with tall bay-windowed terraced houses overlooking a little park and bowling green. Number 49 had a pillar-box-red door with a tidy garden and large sash windows with window boxes of bright purple and yellow pansies, their big petal heads bobbing gently in the breeze. I hesitated before knocking on the door. If things had turned out differently, if Stella had married Michael, this could have been my house, my life, an alternative existence.

I rang the doorbell and heard it chime out a jangly tune. When the door opened I was greeted by two smiling faces. 'You found us okay then?' said Michael.

'Yeah, no problem, my mum gave me directions and it was easy enough.'

Caroline came forward. 'Hi, Tara, come on in, can I take your cardigan?' she asked.

I offered her the bunch of yellow tulips I had bought at Stella's insistence as a hostess gift. 'No thanks, I'm fine,' I said, meaning I wanted to keep my cardi on.

'They're lovely,' said Caroline, smiling as she took the flowers, the intense yellow of the tulips lighting up her face.

'Well, Tara, come on and meet the rest of the family,' Michael said, directing me into the front room.

***

I have met my long-lost family. Not exactly lost, more unknown, but still, now I can actually consider myself part of a family. To think wasn't so long ago that in French class when asked '*Avez-vous des frères ou des soeurs?*', I had to answer '*Non, je suis un enfant unique.*'

Caroline, that's Michael's wife and my editor, was really lovely and welcoming. She worked as a feature writer for the *Belfast Telegraph* when she met Michael but stayed home to look after Beth and Maya when they were little before going back to work. She got the editor job at *Kiss* last year.

Beth has long, silky, ash blonde hair but Maya has my gingery red hair – LOL. We both laughed, looking at how it was virtually the exact same shade of ginger nut biscuits. Beth made us put our heads together to compare and everyone agreed, you couldn't tell the difference.

We had dinner together. Michael ordered in Thai takeaway and we played twenty questions to try to speed up the getting to know each other process.

What's your favourite colour? If you were an animal what would you be? Which countries have you visited? And so on. I can't remember all their answers but at least it was a good icebreaker and a way of relaxing everyone.

When I came home Stella had plenty of questions of her own. Like what did Caroline's house look like and did she make me welcome? Methinks she may be a tad jealous.

Chapter 35

Operation contact

Tara
Sunday 3.09pm

Food supped: porridge, steak with chips followed by chocolate fudge cake courtesy of eating out at a new restaurant with Stella.

Lonely Girl Blog

Much excitement at school since we have Ghoulie Grabber for our form teacher. He is known for his tendency to go off on one and then need a sick note for stress. It was rumoured that he once grabbed a boy by his ghoulies in anger, hence the nickname.

Sat beside Freya in French. We had to introduce each other to the class in French and she said I was *très jolie et* her *ami*!

Matt is even more cracked over Jessica. He said he cannot go through year ten without having some sort of *contact* with her. So we put a plan together to help him in his quest.

Spent yesterday stalking Jessica to enable Matt an opportunity to speak to her without her BFFs. We thought that if we staked out her house we would eventually catch her on her own and he would stride over to her and just do it. Ask her out on a proper date – just the two of them – or if courage failed him altogether he could say me and Ollie would go with them.

We hid behind an Audi A4 for about half an hour outside her house, trying to look anything but suspicious. When Jess finally made an appearance I nudged Matt into action. This was his chance; Jessica Bailey was for once alone, without her friends who acted as buffers between her and him.

'Shit, shit, shit,' Matt said, crouching down behind the car. 'You go, say I asked you to do it for me,' he pleaded.

I gave him the mad evil eye that works so well for Stella and tutted.

'Matthew Jameson, either you go straight over to her right now or I swear to God I will tell everyone in school how you only have one ball.' I hadn't sat there for ages and gained a dead leg for nothing.

'I don't have only one ball.'

'Yes, but who would believe it? Now go!' I watched like a proud parent sending their child off on their first day at school. Jessica had reached near the top of the street before Matt caught up with her. I couldn't hear what he was saying but at least they were talking and walking along. I picked up my jacket which I had been sitting on for the best part of an hour and headed in the opposite direction. I didn't want to play the gooseberry.

Chapter 36

The logic of faith

Wednesday 23rd September 6.08pm

Food nibbled: apple, strawberry yogurt, cheese sandwich and one glass of orange juice.

Gran is asleep in the next room. She has been very poorly and the Marie Curie nurse has told Mum to be prepared. How can you be prepared to say goodbye to someone you love? I try to pretend that I am unaware of what is happening. I don't want to have to talk about Gran leaving us. Skipper sits by her side and looks like someone has stolen his favourite squeeze toy. I know how he feels.

Last week she told me to say a prayer to St Francis for her. I said, 'But doesn't he just do the animals?'

She tried to laugh – it came out like a watery gurgle – and said, 'But sure aren't I an old bat?'

I asked her how she can have such faith when God lets people we love suffer and die. She said, 'How do you know God isn't just about to relieve my pain by taking me up to heaven?' Can't argue with her logic.

Michael has organised a trust fund for the shelter. He recommended a solicitor to take on the paperwork to help sort out the council morons. This was a great suggestion as we now have someone overseeing the trust fund and looking into ways to set the shelter up as a proper charitable foundation. I suggested that we write to Bill Oddie to be a patron. It would be so cool if he agrees.

Michael and Caroline have given a home to one of the last dogs in the shelter, Alfie. He is a blue-grey scruffy sort of mongrel and utterly adorable. Beth and Maya love him to bits. Maya told me she loves having me as a part-time big sister. I wish I could say Beth is as thrilled, but Michael says I need to give her time. After all, until last month she was his oldest daughter and now I have come along and altered the dynamics of her family. I didn't like to point out to Michael that I was here all along, just that he didn't include me as such. I thought I'd better keep that to myself.

Lonely Girl Blog

Kveta and Petar will take over the day-to-day work with the remaining animals. The solicitor is also looking into Petar's immigration case and hopes that since he has served his community service time in Croatia the officials will allow him to work here legally at the shelter since he can say he has somewhere to live. He is staying at Gran's since we don't want her house to be left empty and we can keep the shelter ticking over with Petar there.

Mum has set up the St Francis Animal Sanctuary website. We have an adoption scheme and even fostering for families who can't commit to taking on a pet permanently.

Apparently, Granddad had an insurance policy which left quite a bit of money for Gran when he died, but she had become used to living on very little so it has been lying in a building society account collecting interest. When Gran dies it will transfer to the sanctuary to help keep it running. We have all sorts of fundraising activities planned and Ollie says his dad will sort out a sponsorship deal with his firm.

Beth and Maya come by every Sunday to volunteer. Maya is still too little to walk the dogs but she gives the cats plenty of attention and is helpful at feeding time. Beth and me like to do the walking together. It gives us a chance to talk and get to know each other. I keep hoping that she will become like my bezzie mate – not that I don't still consider Matt a really good BF, it's just that

Beth, being a girl, can fill in the bits of conversation that I miss out on with Matt, like bras, periods, mothers.

My wrist still aches but it's not so bad. The cast will come off next week. Matt asked to sign it and scribbled rude things on it which I had to draw over with my left hand. My artwork has had to go on hold and my word count is way down on my projected count. So frustrating. Tried to dictate to Kveta but she kept interrupting to ask stupid questions like was this really necessary if it wasn't for homework. She said in her village if you didn't have schoolwork you spent your time in the woods snogging boys and smoking and downing quarts of vodka. Such a good role model.

Note to blog reader Space Hopper: I can report that your suggestion worked. I passed you advice on to Matt and we staked out Jessica's house to catch her away from her girl pals. After some persuasion from me, i.e. threats, Matt asked her to go out with him. She did keep him hanging on, all the way to the top of the Lisburn Road, while she considered the prospect. But as hard to get as she played it, they came to an agreement – that we make it a double date. Matt is bribing Ollie and me to come along to make up the foursome. Just wish Ollie hadn't needed to be bribed and asked me out himself. Still, we are going into town for lunch on Saturday afternoon and will spend the day hanging around.

Chapter 37

Playing gooseberry on the Big Wheel

Tara
Saturday 26th September 7.10pm

Food munched: Weetabix with milk, pizza and salad with Coke, will be eating Chinese takeaway soon.

Lonely Girl Blog

Went on Matt and Jessica's big date. We settled on going to Ruby Blue's for lunch. It is a small diner in the city centre located in Queen's arcade and it was full of couples and families stopping for lunch before going shopping.

We queued up to choose our food at the counter and then made our way round the counter to the tills to pay. Matt reached over and gave the girl a ten-pound note and said, 'Take for ours together.' Jessica smiled at him and said thanks. I of course paid for my own and carried my tray to a free table.

'Isn't this the place that was closed down last year coz it was overrun by rats?' asked Ollie when we were settled at our table, completely unperturbed that there might ever have been rats running across the surface.

Matt gave him a dirty look. He didn't want anyone ruining his day with Jessica. 'Yeah, but that was when it was a bakery and the council shut it down. It has since been sold and taken over by new management.' He said all authoritative like he had personally investigated before bringing Jess here.

Matt sat opposite Jessica and offered her a piece of his pizza. She accepted and took a dainty bite, smiling at him from under her thick mascara-coated lashes. I caught Ollie's eye and we shared a conspiratorial smirk.

Later we paid to go to on the Big Wheel at the City Hall. As the capsule rose up into the sky Matt turned to Jess and made his move in, putting his eager lips on hers. Ollie elbowed me in the ribs. 'He's well in there,' he whispered, close enough for me to feel his warm breath on my cheek but nothing else. Anyway, there we were way up above everything, admiring the view when Matt and Jess start snogging. Ollie never made a move on me so we sat there like two gooseberries waiting for the rotations to end.

In London they call it the London Eye but people in Belfast like to call a spade a spade as Gran would say so here it is simply called the Big Wheel (see the Balls on the Falls for another example.)

Stella

It is Joni's fault that I have a hangover. She insisted on pouring me extra-large glasses of gin as we dissected my life.

I sank into her soft pale silver sofa and clutched a Mongolian curly haired cushion while I unburdened the upsets of my recent life. Joni sat with her mouth in a little prim pout, enjoying every minute of my catastrophes.

1. Deranged mother: v sick
2. Ex-boyfriend back in life and has wonderful wife and beautiful daughters
3. Current boyfriend: too young
4. Daughter: in emotional turmoil as I have upended her very existence by springing a previously absent father on her (see point 2)

5. Hiding an eastern European in my spare bedroom because I am too frightened of the Wildling au pair to throw him out

It's a Sunday so I'm going to declare it a *Gilmore Girls* marathon duvet day. I need time with Tara and recuperation.

Chapter 38

Farewell to a good friend

Tara

Food eaten: hardly anything – just a few biscuits, glass of milk and an apple

The rain fell in a veil of soft drizzle as we stood silently around the opened earth. A pile of freshly dug soil lay heaped in a mound to the left. No one knew what to say but there was a sense that the occasion required someone to make a short speech.

Ollie squeezed my hand tightly, just to let me know he cares and that he understands. I bit down hard on my bottom lip, willing myself not to cry. I didn't want to start blubbering in front of everyone, no matter how sad I feel. After a few moments, when it was clear no one was going to speak, Petar made the first move.

'Farewell to a good friend and companion.' He lifted the long-handled spade and began shovelling the clumps of dark soil back into the deep hole. Sometimes words were not enough.

Nora couldn't attend Skipper's funeral but she is recovering well. Her oncologist said that the cancer is retreating and though he couldn't say she was in remission, he was at least confident that the chemotherapy had been effective and worthwhile.

Nora told him there were times when she felt so weak and sick that she felt like telling him where to stick his amber bag of chemotherapy. He said he was glad that she no longer needed his services; she said she was glad to see the back of him too. I think it's a love–hate relationship or, as Gran put it, necessity is the mother of tolerance.

Thought Nora would have been heartbroken over Skipper but she just said that when you get to her age you see beauty in death just as much as in life. Weird thing to say but strangely comforting.

She said Skipper would be waiting for her on the other side along with Granddad and all the other animals she had lost over the years. 'Your granddad will have plenty to say about so many pets but he'll just have to put up with them,' she said.

Maybe St Francis will give her a special award when she gets to heaven for all the work she has done in his name.

It was so tragic to find Skipper lying deathly still at the bottom of Nora's bed but as Mum said he died knowing he had been a good friend to Nora when she needed him most.

***

Nora is feeling stronger today. We went for a walk when I came home from school, the autumn sunshine was too nice to miss out on, and dropped in to see how Petar and Kveta were getting on at the shelter. It is as busy as ever. Stella said Nora needn't think of moving back there, as she wants to keep an eye on her in case she falls back into her old habits of not looking after herself. Nora rolled her eyes but I could tell she was secretly pleased.

On our way to the shelter Nora told me that when Skipper came to her nearly eleven years ago her heart went out to him coz he only had three legs. He had been run over by a bin lorry and had to have his back leg amputated. When all the other dogs came and went she decided that she'd never part with Skipper coz he was just like her – he had a bit missing. When I looked at her like she was off on one of her mad ramblings, she smiled and said, 'You and your mum were my missing bit.'

Maybe St Francis will sort out a new leg for Skipper in heaven.

Chapter 39

Born free

Food gazumped: Three rounds of cheese and toast, wedges with club sandwich and club orange, Thai fried rice and spring roll.

Climbed into the RSPCA van and put my seat belt on.
'Are you ready to do this?' asked Neil, the man from the RSPCA.
'Yeah, she has to go back sooner or later and I know she will be happier in her natural habitat. Who knows, maybe she had pups dependant on her,' I said, trying to keep my voice neutral and even-toned. Bad enough that my eyelids were red and swollen from crying all morning.

Petar, Ollie and Matt followed behind in the van bought with money released from the St Francis fund. Now Petar is able to respond to calls and go collect any stray animals looking for a home. The sanctuary is fully up and running again. UTV have even done a segment on it and interviewed Nora. The house has been refurbished and part of the garden paved to allow for easier cleaning of the hutches.

It has been a wet week with rainfall causing floods all over Belfast. The banks of the Lagan were high and had threatened to spill over onto the towpath. We walked deep into the woodland, away from the weekend walkers who were out for a stroll. Neil and Petar took turns to carry the cage holding the distressed and fearful Roxy.

Every now and then Petar would say, 'Steady, girl, steady, it will be okay.' With help from Kveta and me and the Kardashians, his English is coming on.

Once we were sure we were far enough away from the ramblers we put the cage down carefully at the edge of the forest. The dense trees created a dark cover shielding us from the light rainfall.

'Right, here goes,' said Neil. He lifted the latch and drew back the wired door over the cage. Roxy took a second to sniff the air before edging out ever so slowly. She turned and looked at me, as if to say, is it okay?

'Go on, girl,' I said, and with that Roxy took off. She ran through the trees, her reddish-brown bushy tail trailing behind her.

Chapter 40

Signing off

Sunday

Food consumed: scrambled eggs, wholemeal toast, roast beef and mashed potatoes with cabbage and gravy, pavlova, and one packet of chtereese and onion crisps with a can of Coke.

Lonely Girl Blog

As I type, Gran is sitting in our garden snoozing, with a teal-coloured mohair blanket over her knees. She looks so content and happy, like a proper little granny, all cuddly and warm. I can see her from my bedroom window and can almost imagine that I hear the soft purr of a snore she makes when she sleeps.

There is a smell of bonfires in the autumn air and a sense that there are changes to come. The leaves have turned copper brown and lie in drifts all along the sides of the roads.

Stella has sorted her work schedule so that she spends most of her time in Belfast. It turns out that Belfast is a great place for fashion shoots, lots of gothic buildings for backdrops and zany models all out to make their mark. Stella reckons that Belfast could be the new London, if she hypes it up enough.

We spend more time together now doing things that include Gran. Last Sunday the three of us cuddled up on the sofa with a box of Black Magic and watched *ET*. Stella and me sobbed when it came to the bit where Elliot says: 'You could be happy here, I could take care of you. I wouldn't let anybody hurt you. We could grow up together, ET.'

We recited the lines along with Elliott, tears streaming down our faces, while Gran happily sucked on an orange crème before working her way into the second layer of chocolates.

Dylan McKay got his big part. He is to play George Best in a new biopic of his life. Stella was pleased for him but decided that she didn't want to be seen as a hanger-on and gave him his marching orders.

We had a long chat about her relationship status and how I would feel if she did begin dating in earnest. I said I thought that that was what she had been doing with Dylan, but Stella shrugged as if to say he was small fry. Turns out she is rather embarrassed by the whole Dylan McKay episode and doesn't want to be seen to be doing a Madonna, i.e. seeing a much younger man.

I think Gran is a good influence on Stella. She certainly keeps her in line and can give a mean look if Stella's hemline is too short. Come to think of it, that must be where the mad evil eye originates from! I don't think Gran would approve of Dylan so it's probably better that it has fizzled out.

I think Stella has reflected on some of the things I have said in my column. She no longer criticises everything I choose to wear or the way I style my hair, and she has tried to make excuses for her partying lifestyle and her Dylan period. Last week when we were having a wardrobe clear-out (six black bin bags transported to the Action Cancer shop) she asked me what I thought of her. The question stopped me in my tracks.

I took a second to consider my answer: there was the whole *I hate my mother* phase, *why does she not understand me* and *how can I annoy her?* But I realised that I have moved on. As has she. We seem to accommodate each other more these days. She no longer feels the need to criticise my lack of fashion sense and actually seems proud of my column. She has even asked to see my Cave Dweller sketches and made some suggestions for the subplot.

Her magazine no longer makes me cringe and I actually enjoy rummaging in her wardrobe now, never mind her vast trunk of make-up.

Besides, my friends think she is cool. Yes, I know LOL, I actually have friends! Freya has been hanging out with me as has Jess and some of the crowd. We go up the Lisburn Road and hang out or just chill at each other's houses. Sometimes we let Matt and Ollie tag along but only when we know that they will be cool and not act all weird and silly.

Every now and then Ollie and I get together. He is so sweet and cute and funny. We walk round the park or go to the cinema together and every night he texts me just to say night, night.

Well, this is to be my last entry. The blog will become defunct as of tonight. Lonely Girl is no longer lonely; what with Mum, Gran, Dad, Kveta and Petar, my new half-sisters, my BFFs, and Ollie and Matt around, I am not so lonely anymore.

Thanks for all the input, the comments and suggestions that have been contributed along the way. Certain individuals may be visited by the Sex Pest Police but Spacer, Pop Tart, Jiggy, Diesel, Spoke Wheeler and the rest have been supportive and helpful.

Until next time.

Lonely Girl signing off X.

Acknowledgements

Special thanks to Neil Ranasinghe, Joan McClelland and Katie Kelly for being my first readers.

I am forever grateful to the book bloggers, booksellers and readers who support my books and help to spread the word.

Thanks also to the Bombshell team, Betsy, Fred, Sumaira, Heather and my fellow Bombshell and Bloodhound writers.

I've a great gang of friends. Andrea, Carmel, Katie, Joan, Deborah, Donna, Janette, Roma and Zoe – you are the best gang of personal cheerleaders I could ask for.

Thanks also to writers Sharon Owens and Claire Allan for being so generous with their praise and support.

Finally, to my writer friends who have helped me along the way, thanks for the support and for understanding the moments of panic, especially Sharon Thompson.

Lightning Source UK Ltd.
Milton Keynes UK
UKHW012327050921
389987UK00004B/1096